Seduction

Also by Geneva Holliday

Groove

Fever

Heat

Sugar

The Warmest December

This Bitter Earth

Loving Donovan

Camilla's Roses

Nowhere Is a Place

Seduction

Geneva Holliday

BROADWAY BOOKS

New York

"This is for every Black woman who ever had
a problem with a Black man!"

MADEA,
Diary of a Mad Black Woman

Part One

✦

Part One

CHAPTER

One

Tony Landry slipped the key into the lock and pushed the door open on its hinges. Like a gentleman, he stepped aside and allowed Valerie to step into the apartment first.

He took a moment to marvel at Valerie's long chocolate legs, which seemed to move in slow motion beneath the red crinkled crepe dress she wore. Although referring to it as a dress was a bit of a stretch, since the hem barely hit the curve of her thigh and the plunging neckline hardly covered her areolas.

"This shit is tight!" she squealed as she glided across the khaki-colored area rug toward the west wall and the Charley Palmer original that hung there.

Tony stepped in and pulled the door closed behind him.

She was a beauty; that point could not be denied. So beautiful that he, the great Tony Landry, with all of his confidence and the three hundred plus notches on his belt, had felt a sliver of insecurity crawl up his spine in the moments before he made up his mind to approach her at Perks.

That was three hours ago and in that time he'd dazzled her with his smile, charm, and bootleg Rolex. When he excused himself to go to the restroom, he made sure to hitch his pants a bit so Valerie could see that not only was he good-looking, intelligent, and funny—but he also had a big dick.

Her eyes had bulged, and the tiny bit of a smile she'd been favoring him with grew, and he knew he had her.

"Yeah, it's okay I guess," he said, tossing the keys onto the mahogany sofa table. "Can I get you something to drink?"

It was more than okay. Valerie had said it best: it was tight. Market rent for the apartment would have been a staggering $3,500 a month, but his childhood friend Zebby Trotman had bought it years earlier for a song.

Zebby was a career criminal, and two years ago he got himself mixed up in an international banking scam. Now he was serving time in an Australian prison.

He'd given Tony a spare set of keys to the apartment before the government extradited him. Zebby told Tony he could use the place whenever he wanted. Well, his exact words were: "You can fuck there, but don't think about moving in."

Valerie sat daintily down on the couch, crossing those legs that went on forever, and said, "Champagne?"

She was gliding her index finger up and down the space between her breasts, which he had decided were D cups and real. It was a game he enjoyed playing with himself: Guess Her Bra Size. Sometimes he was wrong and when the bra came off it was padded. But those, those looked real. He could already feel his dick turning to granite.

"Sure," he said, and started toward the kitchen.

He was a player with a capital P. But he was also broke, so he had come up with the bright idea to buy the ten-dollar bottle of Cordon Negro champagne and pour its contents into the one Cristal bottle he'd lifted from some party he'd attended.

By the time he got the women up to the apartment they were usually more than a little tipsy and didn't even know the difference. The popping sound he made with his own mouth.

He opened the cherry wood cabinet and pulled one crystal champagne flute from the shelf. He wasn't a big champagne drinker, and anyway, even if it was just ten dollars a bottle, he couldn't afford to waste any on himself. Tomorrow was another day, and that usually meant another woman.

He walked back into the living room; in one hand he held the crystal flute, in the other, the bottle of Cristal.

A deep look of satisfaction settled on Valerie's supermodel face as her eyes lit on the bottle. "Cristal— hmmmm, you've got real class."

"Thank you," he said as he handed the flute to her and took a seat beside her. She sipped, still marveling at the apartment, before turning to him and asking, "You're not having any?"

Tony shrugged his shoulders. "Work tomorrow," he said, and reached for one of the four remotes on the table and pointed it at the Bose stereo system. The apartment was suddenly filled with smooth jazz.

Valerie gave him a naughty smile and leaned back into the cushions of the couch.

"Nice," she moaned.

He reached for the other remote and pointed it toward the switch panel on the wall and the lights dimmed.

"Damn," Valerie said, turning to him and licking her luscious lips. "You tryin' to get some?" She laughed.

The trying had started at the bar, when he offered her a lift home to Brooklyn and she accepted, and the trying part had come to an end. He knew he had her, hook, line, and sinker.

"Of course not," he said as he reached for her hand and brought it to his lips. He kissed her palm and then the tips of all five digits. "Why would you think that?" he asked as he gave her a mischievous look.

Valerie's eyes narrowed seductively. "You are some kind of man, aren't you?"

Yes, he was some kind of man, but not the kind she thought he was. Tony Landry was a fake, a liar, and a user. Some people would say that he had an insatiable appetite for sex, and that wasn't too far from the truth, but the people closest to him—his mother, his sister, his oldest friend, and Zebby—would tell you that what really got Tony Landry's dick stiff was money.

His father had left him, his mother, and his baby sister when Tony was just eight years old. His mother cleaned hotel toilets to keep the rent paid and food on the table, and some months they ate beans and toast for breakfast, lunch, and dinner.

Clothes, a necessity for most people, became a luxury for the Landry family. They shopped at thrift stores, and Mama Landry was good for rummaging through the Salvation Army clothes bins for outfits for herself and her children.

Tony knew poor and still knew it. His mother had eventually remarried, and things got a little better, but not by much. The husband that had said I do with fourteen years of driving the Metro-North suddenly went blind from diabetes, and the $75,000-a-year salary he was making suddenly dwindled to $1,200 a month in disability payments.

Tony's sister, Janet, had gotten a scholarship to Harvard, while Tony ended up at Borough of Manhattan Community College. Two years later, he was pushing a mail cart at Binge and Beckett Investments. Two years after that he was cold calling for new accounts, and then he was gopher for the top traders at Merrick, and finally an analyst for Jackson Hewitt.

With each new position and salary increase, he'd received a new credit card and commenced to spend like there was no tomorrow, or at least no next month billing statement.

Now he was sixty thousand dollars in debt and had to return home every night to hear his mother complain about the bill collectors that had called the house all day long. Yes, he still lived at home with his mother. Still slept on a twin bed fitted with Superman sheets.

So to Valerie's question "You're some kind of man, aren't you?" Tony grinned wickedly and said, "Yes, I am," as he slowly removed the flute from Valerie's hand.

"Oh," Valerie muttered, a bit flustered.

Tony leaned in slowly, closing his eyes just as his lips pressed against hers. Valerie's lips parted immediately, readily receiving his tongue, a sure sign that when it came time, her legs would do the same.

He pushed her sideways until her head lay atop the armrest; he kissed her neck, the space between her breasts. He would not touch her breasts, wouldn't even let his chin graze them—no, he would wait to be invited. She would have to guide him to them and any other concealed body part. He'd smother her in passionate kisses, tease her earlobes with his teeth, run his tongue across her wrists, suck her fingertips, and massage her shoulders and her waist.

She was moaning and releasing small, breathless cries of pleasure. He took her hand and guided it down between his legs. He was as hard as steel—her palm brushed across his penis and he shuddered while she let out a loud gasp of surprise. Yes, he had a big dick, damn near twelve inches of cock. So big that its size was obvious through his off-the-rack suit slacks, and forget about his jeans, though his casual shirts were long enough to cover the faded imprint his dick left in his blue denims.

It was long, it was thick, and it curved to the left, often leaving the right ovary of the women he bedded a bit sore, and one woman had claimed that he'd knocked it completely out of place.

"*Shiiiiiiiiiiit,*" Valerie hissed as she clutched his rock hard erection, and then added, "Oh my God."

"Baby," Tony breathed into her ear, "no need for formality here. You can just call me Tony." He chuckled.

After that the dress came off and then the thong. She was as bald as a newborn baby down between her legs, and her clitoris was so engorged that it stuck out at him like a bright pink tongue.

He could have done her right there on the couch, but Zebby would kick his ass from here to Xanadu if he came home to fine his expensive couch stained with chick spit and cum. And besides, Tony needed to recork the champagne and get it back into the fridge before it lost its fizz.

He hadn't even undone the top button of his shirt when he pulled himself off her and said, "I'll meet you in the bedroom."

"Okay, baby." Valerie's response was guttural and she gave him a sultry look before she pulled herself up off the couch—naked except for her red stilettos—and sashayed toward the bedroom. At the last minute he found he couldn't resist the urge to slap her ass as she slid by him. Her behind, round, high, and plump, jiggled wildly beneath the assault. Tony's mouth began to water.

When Tony walked into the bedroom, Valerie was lying out on the king bed, propped up against the pillows; her legs were open, knees up in the air, and head thrown back in pleasure as she rolled her clitoris between her fingers.

She spotted him and breathlessly said, "I couldn't wait for you."

Tony watched from the doorway, his penis straining so hard against his pants that when he looked down he could see the silver teeth of the zipper.

He walked toward her, slowly stripping out of his clothes. When he arrived at the foot of the bed, he was buck naked. Creeping onto the bed like a stalking beast, he eased his face down between Valerie's legs, using his nose to nudge her fingers away, replacing them with his eager tongue.

Valerie's back arched and she grabbed hold of his head and cried out in pleasure. Tony felt her warm juices wash over his lips. His dick pulsated with excitement. He loved eating pussy, loved women to squirm and whimper as he sucked and licked them to climax.

Tony lifted his head and took a deep breath before diving in again. He opened his mouth and closed it over her vagina.

Valerie squealed with pleasure as Tony did what Tony did best.

Two minutes later, Valerie reached the most mind-blowing climax she'd ever had, one that forced her eyes up into her head and left her legs flapping together helplessly, like broken wings.

CHAPTER

Two

Mildred always thought her friend Seneca was a little off in the head, about two eggs shy of a dozen. But now what she'd just shared with her confirmed it for sure.

"He did what?" Mildred asked in amazement. Nothing was wrong with her hearing—she had bad eyes, yes, but her hearing was perfect.

"It's called a golden shower," Seneca breathed. "It's very erotic."

Mildred didn't know about that. Erotic? How could somebody pissing on another person be erotic?

"That's just plain nasty."

Seneca rolled her eyes, twisting the sheet of paper towel she held until it was cigarette thin, then began snaking it between her toes. She reached for the bottle of nail polish, Heathen Red.

"It's not nasty, it's sexy," Seneca spouted matter-of-factly as she dipped the brush into the blood red nail polish and then carefully smeared it across the nail of her big toe.

"I'm sure there's a law on the books that states pissing on another person is illegal." Mildred laughed and rocked back and forth on the faded brown catastrophe of a couch that had belonged to her parents before the fatal car accident that claimed them both seven years earlier.

"Shut up, Mildred," Seneca breathed, and started on the left foot.

It was just May and it was already humid. The tiny one-bedroom apartment located on the third floor of 300 Sullivan Place in the Crown Heights section of Brooklyn was steamy, and the windows—all five of them—were thrown open and allowing the late spring heat in.

Mildred had lived in the apartment for four years. Seneca had been an on-again, off-again roommate. For now she had her own place a few blocks away on Lincoln Road, but who knew how long that would last, as she was in the habit of not paying her rent in favor of treating some new lover to a weekend in Vermont. She loved the maple syrup there; she'd confided in Mildred and shared the million and one sexual uses she'd found for it. Mildred, in turn, immediately lost her love for pancakes.

The space was small, barely 350 square feet. You couldn't turn around in the kitchen or the bathroom without bruising your hip bone, and the bedroom would have been considered cozy but the double bed and set of dresser drawers made it cramped instead.

The living room was the largest space in the apartment, and Mildred had given it an airy feel by having the walls painted a creamy yellow and hanging sheer curtains on the two windows that looked down onto the backyard.

"So do you want to catch a movie after?" Mildred asked, stretching herself out on the couch and staring up at the cracks in the ceiling.

"Nah, got a date." Seneca's response was a bit too cheery for Mildred's liking. She bit down hard on her lip until she tasted blood, punishing herself for the jealousy that was biting at her belly.

"Oh."

Seneca called them dates, but Mildred knew that they were something less than that. They were just "fuck meets," which was how Seneca sometimes referred to them. She'd meet up with someone somewhere, have a few drinks, and then take him back to her place or she would go to his place or a hotel and fuck.

Seneca, round, short, and stout, had somewhat of a pretty face if you looked at her sideways and in dim light, but most men thought she was doggish-looking. Mildred knew that for a fact—she'd heard the man in apartment B2 say it, as well as a woman at the A&P.

Seneca had E-cup breasts. She wobbled when she walked, and if she didn't have that mane of curly black hair to balance her, her twenty-pound tits would have pulled her over and onto her face a long time ago.

She was as sweet as pie and funny as all get-out, but she

could be crass at times, and after two drinks she was down-right rude and raunchy.

"So what you gonna do?" Seneca asked as she scruti-nized the job she'd just done on her toes.

"Nothing, I guess," Mildred said, and closed her eyes, blocking out the ceiling cracks.

"Nothing" was her life. She worked Monday through Friday as an assistant to James Henderson, one of the head honchos over at Greene Investments.

Fifty-two thousand dollars a year and three weeks' vacation.

She never took vacation. Well, she took it, because she had to, but she never went anywhere. Not that there weren't places she wanted to go—it's just that she didn't have anyone to go with her. Seneca always promised to go, but then when it was time to book and pay, she always ended up crying broke.

One time Mildred even offered to pay for Seneca's half of the travel package, but Seneca declined, offering some lame excuse that left Mildred believing that it wasn't that Seneca didn't want a free trip, she just didn't want a free trip with her.

So Mildred experienced the world through her travel magazines. She had subscriptions to all of them: *Caribbean Life*, *Travel + Leisure*, *National Geographic*, *Travel*—the corners of her apartment were piled high with back issues. Her favorite places, her must-see-before-you-die places, those pages she'd torn out of the magazines and tacked to the walls of the bedroom and bathroom.

She had twenty thousand dollars in her bank account,

not to mention the fifty-seven thousand she'd accumulated in her 401(k). Her dream was to take the savings account money and spend a year traveling the world—well, that was only if she didn't need it for the dream wedding she'd been planning ever since she was eight years old.

CHAPTER

Three

"Mr. Henderson is in receipt of your résumé and is very impressed." The silky voice came from the other end of the line. Tony's eyebrows rose and his cock jerked in his pants.

"He would like to meet with you for lunch on Tuesday. How does one o'clock at Santucchi's sound?"

Tony was speechless for a moment. He looked over his shoulder to see if anybody was watching him. He was sure his eyes were as big as saucers. James Henderson was the managing director of new accounts and acquisitions over at Greene Investments, the oldest black-owned financial firm on Wall Street.

Tony had faxed over his résumé to the human resources department three weeks before. He was confident that he had the experience for the position advertised in the Sunday *Times*, but he'd never expected to be getting a call from the assistant to Da Man!

"Mr. Landry, are you there?" the sexy voice asked.

"Yes," he croaked, and then cleared his throat. "Yes, I'm here. One o'clock would be fine."

"Okay then. Do you have the address for Santucchi's?"

Everyone knew where Santucchi's was located. All of the big-time power brokers lunched there. Santucchi's was to Wall Street what Sardi's was to the Theater District.

"Yes, I do," Tony said.

✦

Tuesday took forever to arrive. Tony had to wait through all day Friday, the weekend, and then a rainy Monday.

He arrived at Santucchi's ten minutes early. His stomach was in knots as he stood in front of the mirror in the men's restroom, straightening and restraightening his tie. He'd run his hands over his hair so many times that now his palms were greasy.

Washing his hands for the fourth time, he caught sight of the time on his fake Patek Philippe. It was two minutes to one.

Tony still had the paper towel in his hand when he rushed out of the bathroom. Mr. Henderson was just being seated. Tony looked wildly around him for someplace to stash the refuse. He thought of shoving it into his pocket, but then a waiter moved past him with a tray of dirty dishes and Tony dropped it into a half-full coffee cup.

His heart was beating a mile a minute. If he got this job, his base salary would be sixty thousand dollars a year. With overtime and bonuses he could easily pull in a cool one hundred thousand.

He took a deep breath, eased up alongside Mr. Henderson, and said, "Mr. Henderson, I'm Tony Landry."

✦

The interview had gone on for two hours.

He was sure he'd asked all of the right questions, and when Mr. Henderson asked what position he saw himself eventually securing within Greene Investments, Tony gave him his most confident smile and said, "Partner."

Mr. Henderson smiled. He himself had pulled himself up and out of Baltimore's toughest ghetto. The son of a drug-addicted mother, he'd spent most of his life in foster homes. When he was sixteen he was a high school dropout and had already been in and out of four juvenile detention homes. It was clear he was headed straight to the penitentiary when his court-appointed lawyer took an interest in him.

He returned to high school and graduated at the age of twenty-one, with honors. A full scholarship to Howard University followed.

He'd been recruited by Goldman Sachs and Deutsche Bank, but in the end took an analyst position with Greene Investments.

Twenty years and countless promotions later, he'd help build Greene Investments into the financial power-house it had become.

The bottom line was, James Henderson was Tony Landry's hero.

"I like your confidence, Tony, I really do" was Mr. Henderson's only comment before he called for the check.

They parted with another strong handshake and Tony walked away from that meeting feeling the most unsure he'd ever felt in his entire life.

✦

Later that day, Tony was still mulling it over as he and his best friend, Errol Payne, played a game of one on one.

"Why you letting it fuck with you, man?" Errol asked as he tried desperately to block Tony's shot.

" 'Cause," Tony breathed, hunched over, clutching the basketball close to his chest, "I really want that fucking job!" he bellowed before he turned, sprang up into the air, and dunked the ball.

"Damn," Errol screeched as he watched Tony swing from the rim with one hand.

"Twenty-one, dawg, I win again." Tony laughed as he dropped back down to the ground, and smacked Errol on his back.

Errol followed Tony back to the splintered wooden bench.

"You probably got it, so stop stressing."

Tony wiped at the perspiration on his brow and then

lifted the sports bottle of Poland Spring water to his lips and took a long swig.

Errol watched out of the corner of his eye as Tony's Adam's apple bobbed up and down as the water slipped down his throat.

"Hey," Errol said as he reached over and gave Tony's collarbone a tight squeeze, "It's cool, man. You gotta start thinking positive."

"Hey, you're the Buddhist here, not me," Tony said, laughing.

CHAPTER

Four

Mildred was cleaning her glasses when Tony walked up to her desk and announced himself.

She looked up from the task at hand and her eyes lit on a dark blur. Not recognizing the voice or the name, she squinted, and then realized that her glasses were still in her hands.

Calmly, she slipped her glasses back onto her face and then looked up again. Tony was grinning down at her, his dazzling white teeth blinding, and Mildred found herself jerking back a bit in her chair. The sudden movement set the chair in motion and she found herself helpless as the chair rolled backward from the desk, stopping with a slight bump on the wooden file cabinet behind her.

He stood about six feet tall, with a deep chocolate complexion, broad shoulders, thick eyebrows, and the longest lashes she'd ever seen on a man. He was movie-star good-looking and Mildred was immediately smitten.

"Oh," she said as she scooted forward again.

Tony kept his smile steady, but he was wondering how a voice so sexy could come out of such an unattractive woman, and wondered further how she had secured a job with his hero. Tony knew that if he were in Henderson's position, he'd have a fox as his assistant. Not this buck-toothed mongrel of a woman sitting before him now.

"Tony Landry," he said again, extending his hand. "I have a three o'clock with Mr. Henderson."

Mildred blushed and took his hand in hers. It was strong, warm.

"Mildred," she muttered in a small voice, suddenly unable to remember her last name.

Tony's eyes moved between his hand and Mildred's face. After a few moments, when it was clear that Mildred wasn't going to let go, he shook his hand loose of her sweaty palm.

Mildred was staring at him, mouth open and eyes wide, as if she'd been struck.

Tony's grin widened—he was no stranger to the effect he had on women. This one, though, wasn't one he would pursue; she was way past homely.

"Johnson," Mildred suddenly spouted, finally remembering her surname, "Mildred Johnson."

Tony nodded and looked impatiently at his watch.

"Please have a seat. Mr. Henderson will be right with you."

Tony watched from the corner chair as Mildred fussed with some loose papers on her desk before rising and walking toward the smoked-glass office door that read

JAMES HENDERSON
Managing Director

As Tony watched Mildred make her way across the gray carpet, he grimaced as Mildred's run-down orthopedic shoes squealed. He couldn't understand how a woman of Mildred's young age could allow herself to look so unkempt. The outfit she wore was something fit for a sixty-something-year-old who'd never had any kind of fashion sense. And the tired ponytail she sported was ragged and he was sure he saw bits of lint clinging to the strands of hair that didn't quite make it beneath the rubber band.

Mildred called over to him, "You can go in now."

"Thank you," Tony said as he sauntered past her and into the office.

Mildred pulled the door shut and then happily inhaled the lingering scent of his cologne. Delicious—she knew the scent well. She'd been spraying it onto her pillowcases every payday, right before she settled down and dialed 1-800-Hot-Boyz.

Back at her desk, she waited anxiously for Tony to reappear. When he did she called to him, "Have a nice day."

"You too, um . . . Mildred," Tony threw over his shoulder without looking at her.

Mildred melted into her chair. She was in love.

CHAPTER

Five

Errol had stopped going into the Black Swan when he took his vow of celibacy. It was just too many pretty, long-legged temptations in one place.

A few years ago, not unlike Tony, he'd been a whore-monger. Then a friend of his had introduced him to the Buddhist practice. Although he could not find the time to attend the meetings, he studied the religion on his own and began dutifully chanting every morning and evening.

Celibacy had been a hard road to walk, but he made it through every difficult day by whacking himself off.

He'd expertly managed to avoid the Black Swan for months, but he found it hard to say no when Tony called and told him he'd gotten the job with Greene Investments and wanted him to meet him there for a celebratory night out.

Thursday nights at the Black Swan were always good. Wall-to-wall people packed the normally all-white after-work spot. White folk who didn't know that Thursday night was black night could often be seen exchanging confused looks with one another and either sitting back and enjoying the vibe or paying their tab and hustling out the door toward more familiar territory.

Tony was a regular at the Black Swan, and had bedded quite a few women who hung out there. But today would mark the beginning of a whole new set of females, because it was the beginning of summer and the beginning of summer meant a flock of fresh-faced top-college-recruit interns, book-smart Ivy Leaguers who were so green that Tony almost felt bad taking advantage of them.

A twenty-something female was helpless beneath his charm, and if he was on his best game, he could have a new woman beneath him almost every night from June to August.

"What you drinking, man?" Tony turned to him. Errol looked up into his face, but his eyes were on a woman who was standing a few feet away from them.

"Damn, she's got perfect dick-sucking lips," Tony said in Errol's ear, leaning in close.

Errol reluctantly turned his head in the direction Tony indicated. The woman, barely twenty-two from what Errol could see, was smiling in their direction.

"First victim," Tony whispered, and then started toward her.

Errol watched from his place at the bar as Tony made his approach. After ten minutes or so, the woman was tracing Tony's cheekbone with the long pink nail of her index finger. Ten minutes more and Tony was kissing her neck as she giggled girlishly and halfheartedly tried to push him away.

Tony turned toward Errol and winked at him. Errol knew that wink. It was the sign to let him know that Tony was in like Flynn and that their night together was over.

Errol sighed, drained his glass, and threw a twenty down onto the bar.

CHAPTER

Six

Mildred had access to all types of files. She wasn't a dishonest person, really she wasn't, but when Mr. Henderson announced that he had just hired Tony Landry, she just had to know everything about him. And so she pulled his personnel file.

Unmarried.

No children.

A sister.

A mother.

Father deceased.

Age: 34.

She scrolled through page after page of information. They'd hired him even though his credit score was in the 500s and he had a few judgments against him.

Tony Landry was probably something real special for them to ignore that.

Mildred logged off and crossed her fingers.

She had dreamed about Tony Landry the night after he walked into her office. Mildred believed wholeheartedly in her dreams, and she took this particular dream as a sign that they were meant for each other.

Now all she had to do was convince him of that.

✦

Seneca was standing in front of the Black Swan; she had on a short pin-striped miniskirt and an off-the-shoulder white peasant blouse that accentuated her mammoth bosom.

She had way too much makeup plastered on her face, and even Mildred had the good sense to know that ice blue eye shadow went out with the breakup of the Supremes.

"What are you doing?" Mildred asked when she approached Seneca, who was holding a clipboard in her hand.

"I'm signing people up for Maverick Movers and Shakers."

"What's that?"

Seneca gave her an exasperated look. "It's like Black Diamonds."

"What's Black Diamonds?"

"Mildred, you really need to get out more, you know that?"

Mildred shrugged her shoulders and pushed her glasses back up onto her nose.

"It's an organization, a black organization that pro-motes networking functions."

"Oh."

Mildred didn't know anything about parties or net-working functions. The only party she consistently at-tended was the company Christmas party, and even then she only stayed long enough to participate in the first round of toasts. By the time the appetizers were served, she was scurrying out the door.

No one ever seemed to miss her.

"You should go in," Seneca threw at her as she turned and shoved the clipboard at a handsome couple. "Are you on the Mavericks contact list?" she asked.

When she turned around again, Mildred was gone.

✦

Mildred thought about him all night, running his in-formation over and over again in her head until it almost drove her mad. Around midnight, she pulled herself from the bed and padded across the floor to the chest of drawers.

There in the bottom drawer, hidden beneath her winter sweaters, wrapped in layers of aluminum foil and tissue, was the black vibrator Seneca had given her as a birthday gift two years earlier.

Mildred had been horrified and had tossed it aside in anger. Mildred's ungratefulness had hurt Seneca, and she'd stormed out of the apartment. They didn't speak for a month.

Mildred had stared at the repulsive plastic contraption

for hours, afraid to touch it—but more afraid to actually dispose of it because there were nosy busybodies in her building and the thought of them finding it was so upsetting to her that she used the dishtowel to fish it from the trash and wrapped it up in tissue and then tin foil before sticking it in her bottom drawer.

It remained there for a year. She and Seneca never spoke of it, and truth be told, Mildred had almost forgot it was even there until one day the apartment above her, which had been empty for more than six months, was finally occupied by a young woman whom Mildred had laid eyes on only two or three times.

Petite and brown, with track-star thighs and Halle Berry features, she screamed when she climaxed.

The first time Mildred heard her she thought the woman was being murdered and had almost dialed 911, but then laughter followed and soon after that the insistent thumping of her headboard.

The tenant before her had had carpet on the floor and something obstructing the vent, but now the sounds came through so clear that Mildred often felt as if the woman was right inside her apartment.

Mildred would pop a bag of popcorn, turn the lights off—all but the small writing lamp—prop herself up in her bed, and listen to the lovemaking sounds as they filtered down through the floorboards.

It left her excited and wet and she often found her hands down between her thighs, playing with herself.

One Friday night, Mildred lay curled up in her bed, surfing the television channels for a good movie to watch when she stumbled onto a commercial that advertised live chats with hot men.

Mildred was mesmerized by the black men who smiled out at her from the television. With perfect teeth, large biceps, and precisely chiseled chests, they invited her to call in for the nominal fee of $4.00 for the first minute and $2.99 for each additional minute.

Mildred didn't know what had gotten into her, but she dialed the number that flashed in red on the screen.

1-800-HOT-BOYZ

She was advised by a computer-generated voice to enter her credit card number. After a few seconds of clicking sounds, she was connected to a man who introduced himself as Bobby.

Bobby had a voice that sounded like that of the famed radio host Vaughn Harper. Deep, inviting, and sexy.

Bobby also had many questions:

Her name?

Did she have a man?

What was her sexual fantasy?

Did she ever have her pussy licked like a lollipop?

Mildred was speechless. But she was wet, and she looked down between her legs to see a large dark spot spreading through the cotton material of her navy blue panties.

"I'm touching myself. What about you?" Bobby asked. "I'm touching myself and thinking of you. My dick is so hard, so fucking hard for you."

Mildred still couldn't find her tongue. All she was able to manage was a few grunts.

"That's okay, you don't have to talk to me. Just put your finger up inside of your pussy . . ."

Mildred felt dirty but couldn't bring herself to hang up the phone.

"Ooooh," he moaned into the phone. "You feel so wet. So fucking wet. I want to ram my cock inside of your pussy palace."

That was it. Mildred slammed the phone down. But for the rest of the night she couldn't stop thinking about Bobby and what it might feel like to have his cock rammed inside her pussy palace.

After that night she'd called the line frequently, speaking to a few different Hot Boyz: Jackson, Jake, and Gregory.

She'd even incorporated Seneca's gift into her sessions with her fantasy men. And now she could bring herself to climax for just under thirty dollars.

But tonight she wouldn't need to call the hotline. She had her real live fantasy man. And so she reached for her vibrator, lay back, closed her eyes, and imagined Tony was pushing his cock into her pleasure palace.

CHAPTER

Seven

"Tonnnnnnnnnny!"

Tony rolled over in his twin bed and pulled the pillow over his head, blocking out his mother's insistent calls.

The bedroom door slammed open. "I know you hear me calling you, boy!"

"What? What?" Tony screamed into the pillow.

His mother, Ethel, walked over to the bed, kicking stray sneakers, comic books, and underwear out of her path as she went.

"There are dishes in the sink, the garbage was never thrown out . . . I came in this morning and the mice were having a picnic!"

Tony rolled his eyes. "Sorry, I forgot."

"You'd forget your head if it wasn't attached to your body," Ethel said, tossing the pillow down to the foot of the bed. "Now get up and do it!"

Tony took a deep breath and peeked over at the digital clock. It was just past eight o'clock in the morning. His mother had no respect for him. He worked hard all week long; all he asked was to sleep in late on Saturdays.

"Christ! That's what you need. You need the Lord in your life!" Ethel was shaking her index finger and bellowing from the doorway.

Tony sighed. "Ma," he murmured as he sat up in the bed.

"What are you going to do with your life? Huh? What?" Ethel glared at him.

Tony got up from the bed, walked toward his mother, and kissed her affectionately on the forehead. "I'm going to do great things. You'll see," he said as he moved past her and out into the living room.

"Really?" Ethel said, pressing her fists into her wide hips. "Well, start with washing the dishes!"

✦

"So what happened with that girl the other night?" Errol asked as he plucked a wheat roll from the breadbasket. He had invited Tony out for a celebratory meal at the Sugar Bar.

"Nothing. I couldn't get her to come back to the spot with me, but I did get her number."

Errol pulled the roll apart and stared into its soft middle. "What was her name?"

Tony shrugged his shoulders as he perused the menu. "I dunno. Stacy, Tracy, something."

Errol shook his head, then something occurred to him. "Oh yeah, man, did you buy your mother a gift?"

Tony dropped the menu and gave Errol a blank look. "What?"

"Tomorrow is your mother's birthday, man. Don't tell me you forgot again."

Tony nodded his head, and then gave Errol a sly grin. Errol knew what that meant.

Errol had been covering Tony's ass in so many different ways and for so long, it had become second nature to him.

When Errol's mother died when he was eight years old, Mrs. Landry had stepped up, filling the void the death of Errol's mother had left behind. So in some ways he thought of Ethel Landry as his mother too and treated her as such.

Tony, so self-absorbed, could barely remember to buy her a card. Errol scolded Tony about this on numerous occasions, reminding him that his mother had taken on a second job cleaning offices at night just to put him through college.

But talking to Tony was often like talking to a wall, so Errol had just given up and now sent an extra dozen roses in Tony's name.

"So you got that for me?"

"Yeah, man. I got it," Errol said.

The meal was wonderful, complete with an expensive bottle of wine, followed by Couvoisier. The bill totaled well over two hundred dollars.

"Thanks, man," Tony said as they exited the restaurant.

"No problem."

They walked along the street in silence. When they got to the lot where Errol had parked his Range Rover, Tony turned to him and said, "You know, man, I think this is the beginning of something big."

Errol couldn't remember ever seeing Tony's face so serious. So earnest.

"I think so too, man."

CHAPTER

Eight

Mildred spent all of Saturday and Sunday milling around her apartment, flipping through her beloved travel magazines and watching the clock, counting the hours and minutes until Monday morning.

She'd put on her best outfit, a pink and brown checkered wool skirt suit, even though it was late May and the weather was too warm for it.

Mildred didn't own a pair of heels; she couldn't walk in them anyway. Whenever she'd make an attempt, by her fourth step she was toppling sideways, falling over like a diseased oak. Mildred's shoe collection was made up of loafers, two worn-out pairs of Nikes, and a pair of pink galoshes.

She never wore makeup, but this time she had made a

special trip to Rite-Aid to buy a tube of strawberry-flavored lip gloss, and she'd done one other special thing for herself that she hadn't done in a decade.

Sunday afternoon, she sat on her bed, an old issue of *Essence* magazine open on her lap as she followed the instructions for a hairstyle that she thought would suit her natural hair. Mildred had a standing press and curl appointment at the neighborhood beauty salon, which was patronized by bent old ladies and kindergartners. For the first time in twelve years she'd canceled her appointment, opting to follow the instructions in the magazine, which required the person to thoroughly wash her hair and then part it into quarters, generously applying protein gel to the locks before braiding them tightly and then pin rolling the hair before sitting under the dryer until it was dry.

Monday morning, Mildred rose at five o'clock, unbraided her hair, and was horrified to find that it was a stiff mess. A bird's nest!

She looked like one of those Africans who swung through the trees in the old black-and-white Tarzan movies.

Crying, she poured cup after cup of water over her head, softening it as best she could before greasing it and then pulling it back into a ponytail.

Black penny loafers spit-shined and gleaming, she straightened the hem of her jacket, lifted her head high in the air, and started out of the apartment and toward her destiny.

CHAPTER

Nine

Tony strolled into 120 Broadway dressed smartly in a gray Armani suit complete with Valentino shades and a copy of the *Wall Street Journal* tucked under his arm.

Taking the elevator to the sixth floor, he stepped out and started toward the receptionist's desk.

The woman was good-looking, with a mass of red hair and long maroon fingernails. She took a quick double glance at Tony and then her face broke into a smile.

"Good morning," Tony said.

"Good morning, sir. How can I help you today?" the woman asked, slowly taking Tony in.

Tony presented his hand. "My name is Tony Landry. I'm the new analyst."

The woman's eyebrow arched. "Really? Which department?"

"Inactive accounts."

"Well, welcome aboard, Mr. Landry."

"Please, call me Tony." Tony smiled and leaned in a bit. "All my friends do," he added, getting a nice peek at her cleavage. "And I hope we'll be good friends."

Already he was treading in dangerous waters, flirting on the first day.

"Cherise," the receptionist said, folding her hands beneath her chin, "but my friends call me Cherry." She winked.

Tony didn't miss the two-carat platinum diamond engagement ring on her finger.

"Lucky man," Tony said, nodding at the ring.

"Don't think he don't know it either." Cherry licked her lips.

They just grinned at each other for a moment until the elevator doors opened and a dozen employees spilled into the corridor.

"Oh," Cherry sounded and raised her hand, waving at someone who'd stepped off the elevator. "Mr. Finkle," she called.

Tony turned around and his eyes fell on a short, balding man with liver spots dotting his face. The suit he wore was wrinkled and hadn't been cleaned since he bought it, judging from the scent wafting from it.

"Yes, Cherise?"

"Mr. Finkle, this is Tony Landry, the new analyst in your department."

Finkle, who stood barely five feet, tilted his head back, scrutinized Tony for a minute, and then offered his hand. "Art Finkle. Sorry I wasn't here to interview you—I was on vacation in Tampa with my family. Had a wonderful time. Got a little sunburned, though, and the wife spent too much money, but the crab legs were the best I've had in Florida. Have you been to Florida? Gonna retire there in five years if this job doesn't kill me first."

Finkle kept shaking his hand the entire time he rambled. Tony fought hard to keep the amusement off his face. When Finkle finally released his hand, he turned on his heels and started toward the office, still in midstream.

Tony looked at Cherry. "You'd better follow him," she said.

✦

Tony's desk was small and in a cubicle. Not at all what he'd imagined or hoped for.

Sighing, he tossed his newspaper down onto the desk and unbuttoned his jacket. Just as he was about to sit down, a young man's face appeared over the edge of the cubicle wall.

"Hey, you the new guy?"

Tony nodded and then offered his hand. "Tony Landry."

"Habib Habib."

Tony gave the Middle Eastern man a quizzical look. He wasn't sure he'd heard right.

"Did you say Habib Habib?"

"Yeah, I know—it's a long story." The olive-skinned man laughed. "Nice to meet you. I'm the senior analyst here, so if you need any help, just holler."

"Thanks."

Tony settled himself down at his desk and turned his computer on. A package with his password, a company manual, and benefits information had arrived on Saturday via Federal Express, and now with horror he realized that he'd left the whole thing at home on his dresser. He had no way to sign in to the system.

Oh, this is going to be a fine first day! he thought to himself.

He gathered his pride, cleared his throat, and stood up. He turned right and peered over the edge down into Habib's cube.

Habib was huddled over his keyboard, already working feverishly away.

"Hey, Habib. I've got a small problem."

✦

Mildred stepped off the elevator and quickly flashed her ID badge at Cherry before scurrying past her and into the office.

She spotted him immediately, talking to the Pakistani guy who'd stumbled over and pinched her behind two Christmas parties ago. She had thought that he was interested and had started to read up on Pakistani customs, but he never even acknowledged her beyond that night. It was as if the whole incident had never happened.

Taking a deep breath, she started toward Tony. Her heart was pounding in her ears and she was perspiring profusely.

When she was one cubicle away from him, her head began to spin. She was losing her nerve—she wasn't ready to approach him. At the last minute she turned quickly around and ran right into an employee who was carrying a tray heavy with Starbucks coffee.

They slammed into each other, sending the coffee flying, most of which ended up on Mildred.

Mildred yelped as the steaming liquid seeped through her suit and onto her skin.

"Oh my goodness," the young man shrieked. "Are you okay? I'm so sorry. I—"

Mildred was horrified. She didn't dare turn around to see if Tony was looking her way. With her eyes filled with tears, she hurried away.

✦

Tony had turned around just as Mildred shrieked. He didn't know who it was that was hurrying away in that awful pink and brown checkered suit, but Habib cleared that up for him.

"Humph," he sounded as he pointed in Mildred's direction. "That's the big man's secretary. Mildred Jackson."

"Oh yeah," Tony responded, remembering her silky voice and awful teeth.

"She had a crush on me a few years ago." Habib grinned proudly.

Tony nodded, then shook his head in dismay.

CHAPTER

Ten

W hat in the world happened to you, Mildred?"
Mr. Henderson demanded when he walked into the
office suite and found Mildred seated behind her desk,
drenched in coffee.

"Oh, I had a little accident," she said, her eyes lowered.

"Well, you can't sit here all day like that. You'll catch
your death of cold under this air-conditioning."

Mr. Henderson was right, of course—her teeth were
already chattering uncontrollably.

"But you have three meetings today and a—"

"And nothing, Mildred. Amy Hicks will cover for
you," Mr. Henderson said.

James Henderson wondered about his assistant sometimes. She was a strange bird and not the most beautiful

woman in the world, but she was efficient and dedicated and had the best phone voice he'd ever heard.

He'd had his share of beautiful assistants who didn't do their job half as well as Mildred. And besides, he was getting up in age and had wrecked two marriages while he was busy screwing his assistants. He'd hired her not only because she came with exemplary references but because he knew that nothing would ever happen between them.

"Go on home, Mildred," he said firmly. "Take one of those sick days you never use."

✦

An hour later, Mildred was back in her small apartment, curled up on the couch, still dressed in her coffee-stained suit, crying herself to sleep.

By noon, her telephone was blaring off the hook and she answered it sleepily.

"Hello?"

"Mildred, what are you doing home?"

The voice was familiar, but Mildred was still trying to climb out of her slumber and couldn't quite place it.

"Who is this?"

"What? Mildred, are you kidding around? It's Geneva!"

Mildred wiped at her eyes and pulled herself up into a sitting position.

"Oh, Geneva, hi," Mildred responded, still groggy.

"I had called to see if you wanted to grab lunch together and some other woman answered your phone and said you'd gone home sick for the day. What's wrong?"

Geneva was a woman who had been temping at the firm for a year. They'd become quite close, taking lunch together most days. Geneva had become sort of a confidante for Mildred. She could share things with Geneva that she couldn't share with Seneca.

"Um, I think I might be coming down with something," Mildred lied, unable to share the embarrassing accident she'd been involved in.

"Really?"

"Yeah, well, it's just a headache. A . . ."—Mildred searched for the word—"a migraine."

"Really?" Geneva didn't sound like she believed her. "Well, did you take something for it?"

"Yeah, I took some Tylenol. I'll be okay. Can I call you later?"

There was a long silence before Geneva spoke again.

"Sure, baby. You call me when you're feeling better."

"Okay, Geneva. Bye."

"Bye."

Mildred hit the End button on the phone and pulled herself up from the couch, stretching her body and yawning. She started toward her bedroom, intent to make use of the day and at least clean out her closet, but a better thought popped into her head.

"Oh, Mildred, you are a sick puppy!" she said to the empty apartment.

She tiptoed to the bed and sat down. Picking up the

phone, she dialed the hotline. She'd called so much that she was now a platinum member, which came with a personal pin number as well as coupons that invited members to peak during the off-peak hours at a discounted price.

Mildred looked over at the clock. It was just past eleven.

Off-peak.

Mildred pulled her vibrator from the drawer, quickly stripped out of her clothes and underwear, and climbed under the covers.

She had Hot Boyz on speed dial, and so she hit the corresponding number and then speakerphone.

Nothing was wrong with a little self-love in the afternoon, now was there?

CHAPTER

Eleven

Errol was standing on the corner of Broadway and John Street talking to a former colleague of his when Tony bounded up.

"Hey," he said, and then nodded at the woman Errol was speaking to.

"Liz Choi, Tony Landry," Errol said.

Tony had never had an Asian woman, and now, looking at the beauty standing before him, he couldn't imagine why he'd never gone down that road.

"Nice to meet you," Tony said, and then quickly added, "You are the most stunning woman I've ever seen."

Liz blushed. "Thank you."

Errol rolled his eyes and then said, "Look, Liz, this guy is dangerous. Watch yourself."

Liz rocked on the heels of her Jimmy Choos and then reached into her pocketbook and fished out a business card.

"Here you go, Mr. Landry," she said as she handed the card to Tony and winked. "I like danger."

Tony's eyebrows rose. He liked her.

Tony tucked the business card safely into the breast pocket of his jacket.

Liz said her goodbyes and was off. Tony and Errol watched her until she disappeared into the rush-hour crowd that was moving like cattle down the street and toward the train station.

"So how was the first week?"

"It was all right, I guess. It ain't exactly brain surgery," Tony said as they started down the street.

"Is that so," Errol said.

"Yeah—I mean, I've been doing this shit for four years now. I can do it with my eyes closed."

Errol nodded as they stepped out of the path of a woman pushing a twin stroller.

"Researching inactive accounts is not the biggest thrill in the world, but hey, it pays the bills."

"So why do you keep doing it? Why don't you move on to something else?"

"I keep doing it because I'm good at it. I had an eighty-five percent success rate at my last job and I hope to increase that at Greene Investments. Do you know what those senior analysts make? Their salary base is six figures and they could double that with overtime and bonuses."

Errol didn't know the inactive accounts part of the business. So he listened intently as Tony rambled on.

"The senior analysts research companies whose activity has been at a standstill for more than six months. You'd be surprised how often that happens. When a small company folds, it's not big news, and so you're not going to read about it in the *Journal*."

"I see," Errol said as they crossed Broadway and headed toward McAdams Bar.

"How many accounts did you satisfy this week?"

"Shit, like thirty-five."

"Is that a lot?"

"From what my supervisor Habib Habib says, it is."

Errol stopped. "Habib Habib? Why are you saying the man's name twice?"

"Long story." Tony laughed. "I'll tell you over drinks."

◆

McAdams was packed with the usual Wall Street crowd. VPs, traders, investment counselors, and administrative staff—they were all there, washing away the week's tensions in alcohol.

Errol and Tony were on their second beer when Cherry the receptionist sauntered up to them. "Hey, Tony."

"H-hey . . . Cherry!" Tony was more than happy to see her.

"So how was your first week?"

"Stellar. Thanks for asking."

"No problem. So who's your friend?" Cherry inquired as she gave Errol a seductive once-over.

"This is my best friend, Errol. Errol, this is Cherry. She's the receptionist on my floor."

"Nice to meet you," Errol said.

"Same here." Cherry's response was breathless. "I guess it's true what they say, huh?"

Tony's eyebrows rose. "What's that?"

"Birds of a feather flock together."

Tony and Errol exchanged confused glances.

Cherry did a slow head toss, sending her mane of red hair cascading over her shoulder. "C'mon—you rarely see two good-looking men together. One is usually a dog."

"I think we've just received a compliment, Errol." Tony laughed.

"I guess we have," Errol said, and then turned to Cherry and said, "Thank you."

"Why don't you thank me properly and buy me a drink?"

Errol's eyebrows arched in surprise at her forwardness.

"Sure, why not? What are you having?"

✦

When Errol finished his third bottle of beer, it was just past ten. He'd paced himself. Tony, on the other hand, had thrown back shot glass after shot glass of Hennessey, and Cherry didn't seem to have a problem keeping up with him.

By the time Errol left the bar, Cherry was propped squarely on Tony's lap, with her tongue darting in and out of his ear.

Errol straightened his tie, tapped Tony on the shoulder, and mouthed "I'm out."

Tony gave him the peace sign.

✦

"Where's the freakiest place you've ever done it?" Cherry whispered in Tony's ear.

"Well, I don't know . . . There's been a few places—"

"Have you ever done it on the subway?"

"Well, no, I don't think so—Ow!" Tony screamed and pushed Cherry off his lap. Cherry had taken nibbling to another level and had bit down a little too hard on his ear-lobe.

"Sorry, baby," Cherry cooed. "Let mama make it better for you," she said, trying to ease back down onto his lap. Tony looked at her, and her lips were glistening with his blood.

"Fuck," Tony mumbled as he jumped up from the chair and started toward the bathroom.

There was blood on his collar and he cussed under his breath as he pressed a wet paper towel to the wound.

"That's one crazy bitch, huh?"

Tony turned to see who had addressed him. It was one

of the other analysts, Jim something or other. Tony couldn't quite remember.

"I had her, you know. Best lay ever," Jim said as he gave his penis a hearty shake before zipping up his pants and walking over to the adjacent sink to wash his hands.

Tony laughed. "Well, good for you—but I'm just having a good time. I'm not thinking about—"

Jim put his hands up, halting Tony in midstatement. "Hey, man, I'm not judging you. It's just that she's all over you like flies to honey, you know? But I want you to know that you're nobody special. I don't want to call her a slut, but she's had some up-close and personal time with most of the cocks in the firm, if you get my meaning." Jim winked before turning to the mirror and sliding his hands over his slicked-back hair.

"Botticelli," Tony murmured to himself. "Jim Botticelli." He laughed. Funny how the guy's name popped into his head as soon as he dragged his hands across his hair.

The bleeding had stopped and Tony knew the right thing for him to do was to walk right out into that bar, say good night to Cherry, and head home.

But Jim Botticelli had said she'd been a great lay. Not *good. Great!* And who was Tony Landry to turn down something as wonderful as that?

✦

They jumped in a cab and headed toward Brooklyn.

Cherry was as drunk as a skunk and extremely

amorous. She'd slipped her thong off as soon as they'd settled themselves into the backseat of the cab.

"Feel how wet you've made me," she purred in Tony's ear as she guided his hand up between her legs.

Tony grinned and pushed his finger up into her moist hole.

Cherry groaned with pleasure as she reached for his belt buckle and began to expertly undo it with one hand. Before he knew it, she had unzipped his pants and had her hand inside the fly of his boxers, wrapped around his dick.

"Hey, hey," Tony admonished when she tried to remove his penis from the safety of his pants. "Let's just simmer down here," he heard himself slur halfheartedly.

The cabdriver's eyes swung eagerly between the road and his rearview.

"I've got to see it. I've got to have it in my mouth," Cherry cried.

"Well, if you put it that way," Tony said.

Cherry sprang back in pleasant surprise. "It's *sooo* big," she cooed with delight.

"Yeah, it is," Tony said proudly, almost not noticing that the cabdriver had forgotten himself and turned around to see for himself.

"Hey, what are you, some type of freak?" Tony barked at him. The cabdriver quickly turned his attention back to the road.

"Go ahead," Tony said, thrusting his pelvis up toward her. "Put it in your mouth like you said you would."

Cherry grinned sheepishly. "But . . . but I didn't know it would be so *biiiiiig!*" she cried girlishly.

The cabdriver chuckled and then quickly cleared his throat.

"C'mon, girl," Tony urged. The tip of his cock was throbbing.

Cherry swallowed, tucked her hair behind her ears, and bent her head to receive him.

Tony watched the bright lights of New York City stream by outside the cab window as Cherry wrapped her succulent lips around his manhood. "Oooh," Tony moaned softly as he gently pressed his palm against the back of her head.

Cherry expertly glided her mouth up and down his phallus while her hand caressed his scrotum. Tony flung his head back in ecstasy and raised his hips, thrusting himself deeper into Cherry's mouth.

"Yes, baby, yes, baby," he panted as he wrapped his fingers tight around Cherry's hair and began to thrust harder. "I'm coming, I'm coming," he whispered.

Cherry pressed her thumb to the base of his penis and used her remaining four fingers to give his scrotum a tight squeeze. Tony had never been done that way before. The result was mind-blowing and Tony couldn't help but cry out in pleasure. "Jesus fucking Christ!" he screamed as he squirted hot semen into her mouth.

It was the best blow job he'd ever received.

Cherry's head popped up and she quickly rolled down the car window and spat his seed out into the night air.

Dragging the back of her hand across her lips, she smiled and asked, "Did you enjoy it?"

Tony nodded his head. He had enjoyed it. "You're the

best," he muttered before his eyes fluttered closed. "By the way, what part of Brooklyn do you live in?"

"Well," Cherry began, cuddling up close to him, "it's not quite Brooklyn. It's actually Howard Beach."

Tony's eyes flew open and he shot straight up. "Did you say Howard Beach?"

Cherry nodded, doe-eyed.

"I can't go to no fucking Howard Beach. Do you know what they do to men that look like me there?"

Cherry levied a playful slap to his arm. "Aw, that's just propaganda."

"Propaganda my ass," Tony said. He leaned forward and shouted through the glass partition, "My man, you can drop me in East Flatbush."

"You're not going to come home with me?" Cherry said, already pouting.

"Nah, maybe another time. Like when it's daylight and I have my Glock with me."

Twelve

Well, are you going to go?"

"I—I don't think so."

"But I wanna go!" Seneca wailed.

"Stop acting like a baby—people are watching."

Mildred and Seneca had stopped at a pizza parlor after a day of roaming around the city; Mildred had stupidly mentioned that the annual company picnic was taking place the following weekend.

"You said you could bring a guest. I want to be your guest—I want to meet an investment banker . . . somebody with some loot!" Seneca squealed as she licked tomato sauce from the corners of her mouth. "And I'm sure that guy you got the jones for will be there too," Seneca added slyly.

Mildred blushed. It had been a month since Tony started with the company and she'd seen him exactly two times. Once at the elevator bank, she was standing right next to him and he didn't even notice her. Another time she was on the street and he was on the corner talking to some guy.

Mildred had spotted him and stopped dead in her tracks as if in a trance. It wasn't until some rude pedestrian pushed her out of the way that she came back to her senses and walked quickly away.

"I don't have a jones for him," Mildred retorted. "I just think he's an attractive man."

Seneca smirked at her. "Well, if you don't want him, I'll take him."

"Shut up!" Mildred shouted. Seneca's statement had hit a nerve. They were friends, but Mildred knew Seneca's track record. She'd bedded her sister's boyfriend back in high school and had laughed it off like it was nothing. Mildred knew that if Seneca could do something like that to family, she herself didn't have a chance.

"Calm down, calm down," Seneca whispered. "I'm just kidding. Damn. Anyway, it's not like the man even knows you exist."

Mildred rolled her eyes at her. What did she know? Mildred had faith—faith that she and Tony Landry would be together one day.

◆

The company picnic was a lavish affair that took place in Central Park on a cloudless, warm June day.

Yes, there were the usual hot dogs and hamburgers, but there was also a rolling raw bar and sparkling wine.

Mildred and Seneca made their way through the throngs of people, stopping at various food stands to sample the delectable offerings.

Mildred even had a glass of sparkling wine, which went straight to her head—the reason she agreed to get her face painted in the first place.

"C'mon, girl, let's do the potato-sack race."

"Have you lost your mind?" Mildred laughed. "I'm not doing that."

"C'mon—the winners get five hundred dollars!"

"I don't care if it's five thousand dollars."

"I'll do it with you," a voice floated over to them.

Mildred and Seneca turned around to see Tony Landry standing behind them. With him was the man Mildred had seen him talking to on the street.

Mildred was stunned and Seneca looked like she was a minute from jumping his bones. Her mouth dropped open as her eyes slowly moved from his face and then stopped squarely on his crotch.

"Sure thing, good-looking," Seneca spouted as she shifted her weight and sucked in her gut so that her already oversize breasts magically expanded in the baby blue tube top that was too small to begin with.

Mildred tried to say something, but her words were caught in her throat and she watched helplessly as Seneca grabbed hold of Tony's hand and started toward the table where the activities sign-up sheets were located.

"That's going to be some kind of race, huh?" Errol

was talking to Mildred, but Mildred still couldn't find her voice.

Errol made a face and then repeated his statement, this time a bit louder. "I said, that's going to be some kind of race!"

Oh God, Mildred thought to herself. He thinks I'm hard of hearing!

She quickly nodded her head yes.

"So, you work for Greene Investments?" he said, moving beside her. "Do you know Tony?"

Mildred's eyes were glued to Tony and Seneca, who were stepping into the sacks.

She shook her head no and then yes.

Errol laughed. "Well, do you know him or not?"

Mildred found her voice, but it was weak. "We met once."

Mildred could feel the stranger's eyes boring into her. And why wouldn't he stare? She was acting like a freak. She turned and met his gaze.

"I'm Mildred," she said.

"Nice to meet you, Mildred. I'm Errol. I like the cat whiskers," he said, pointing to the paint on Mildred's face.

◆

Tony strolled over to Errol and Mildred, shaking both fists triumphantly in the air, shouting, "I rule! I rule!"

Seneca skipped contently behind him, winking at Mildred as she came.

"Now, how much of five hundred dollars are you going to share with me?" Errol asked as he patted Tony heartily on the back.

"You mean two hundred and fifty," Seneca sang. "We have to split the winnings."

Seneca's statement started a light banter between the two of them. Mildred marveled at Seneca's quick wit and her ability to go toe to toe with Tony. At that moment, Mildred felt a deep admiration and hatred for her friend.

"Hey, why don't we all go out and have a real meal, spend some of that found money?" Errol suggested.

Mildred had already started to fade into the background. It seemed to her that she had melted into the crowd and the three of them were yards away on the other side of the open field.

Tony gave Errol a look that said. *Negro, have you lost your damn mind?*

But Errol ignored it and then turned around in search of Mildred.

"Hey, Mildred, what are you doing way back there? Come on—we're going to help them spend their winnings!" he called to her, waving her back into the fold.

"O-okay."

✦

They ended up at a small Thai restaurant on Columbus Avenue. Seneca and Tony sat next to each other and Errol and Mildred sat across from them, Mildred facing Tony.

It was all she could do to keep from staring at him. She

watched his every move and committed it to memory. She had little to say; she was just grateful to be in his company, even if it meant watching Seneca flirt shamelessly with him.

Tony on the other hand tried to make the best of the situation, although it turned out he had to work extra hard at not laughing at Mildred, because the painted whiskers played on her severe buck teeth and made her look like a ghastly rabbit.

Whenever their eyes met, she grinned stupidly before shoving another forkful of food into a mouth that never seemed to close. And he had the strange feeling that she was undressing him in her mind.

When the meal was done and the waiter with the annoyed expression made a fourth approach, inquiring if there was anything else he could get for them, they knew it was time to go.

"Can I give you two a lift to Brooklyn?" Errol offered, even though Tony was giving him that *Are you crazy?* look again.

"No thanks," Mildred squeaked, but she wasn't heard over Seneca's thunderous "Yes!"

They climbed into the plush leather seats of Errol's Range Rover and Seneca looked as if she were going to climax right then and there.

"Damn, Errol, this is a nice ride," Seneca spouted as she moved her hands over the leather.

"Yes, very nice." Mildred just thought she should add that.

The traffic was horrible, and it took them nearly an

hour to get into Brooklyn. Mildred was panicked the entire trip: she didn't want to be dropped off first; if she was, she was sure Seneca would pounce on Tony.

At the last minute and just blocks before they reached her apartment building, she blurted, "Seneca, I need you to come up to my place. I have something I want to show you."

Seneca's head was bouncing happily to Fergie's latest tune. "Can't I see it another day?" she said without looking at her.

"No," Mildred retorted a little too loudly. "I really need you to see this."

Seneca released a long sigh and then leaned over and whispered in her ear, "Why you cock-blocking, Mildred?"

Mildred's heart began to gallop. She felt the hairs on her neck jump to attention and she suddenly found her hand clamped down on Seneca's knee as she spoke between clenched teeth. "It's important, Seneca," she said, giving her a painful squeeze.

"Ow!" Seneca wailed, shoving Mildred's hand away. "That hurt, you know."

Mildred stole a look at the rearview mirror and found Errol watching her.

"Sounds serious," he said with an air of humor.

"Yeah, I guess," Seneca grumbled under her breath.

They stood on the curb, waving as the truck pulled out. Then Seneca turned to her friend, placed her hands on her hips, and said, "Thanks a lot, Mildred. I was hoping to get the digits. That boy was fine!"

Mildred swallowed hard and then looked deep into

Seneca's eyes and said, "That was the guy I've been telling you about."

Seneca's face went blank. "Who, Errol?"

"No!" Mildred screamed, and gave Seneca a rough shove. "Tony!"

Seneca's eyes widened. "Oh," she squealed, throwing her hands over her mouth. "My bad."

Thirteen

Dude, what the hell is wrong with you?" Tony asked, turning to Errol.

"What?"

"You think I wanted to spend my afternoon with those two bow-wows?"

"C'mon, man—aren't you being a little hard on them? They're nice girls."

"That big-titty girl was all over me!"

"Seneca. Her name is Seneca."

"I don't care what the hell her name is. And her friend—"

"Mildred."

"Yeah, Mildred. Goddamn—who knew ugly could be so . . . so . . . ugly!"

"Okay, she's not the best-looking woman in the world, but she's got a real nice personality."

"Whatever, man. All I know is, they cramped my style. Our style. Did you see how the honeys were looking at us? They couldn't believe two good-looking men like us were sitting down to eat with dogs. They probably thought they were our girlfriends!" Tony shivered with disgust. "Don't ever—*ever* put me in that type of situation again. Do you hear me?"

Errol shook his head in dismay.

They rode in silence until the blaring sound of Tony's cell phone shattered it. Looking down at the number, he groaned.

"Who is it?"

"Cherry."

"Cherry the receptionist Cherry?"

"Yeah, man. She's sweating me like you wouldn't believe."

The phone continued to blare.

"Well, are you going to answer it?"

"I can't be bothered, man. What's wrong with women? I told her that we could get down every now and again, but no strings, you know?"

Errol nodded.

"She was all like, Yeah, no problem, I gotta man, I just want to have some fun before I get married—"

"When's that?"

"September or some shit, I don't know. It's not like I got an invitation or anything. But you know, Errol, I fucked this girl twice," Tony said, holding two fingers up for emphasis, "*dos*, and now she's acting like she's all in love."

Errol remained quiet. Tony was thirty-four years old and still didn't understand women. Women had a bad habit of confusing sex with love, and Tony had yet to realize that.

"And dude, what makes it worse is that I gotta see her every fucking day at work!"

"I told you, never eat where you shit."

"Yeah, yeah." Tony laughed and waved his hand at Errol.

"One day you'll learn."

Tony shook his head. "Maybe one day, but not today."

CHAPTER

Fourteen

Oh, shit!" Tony screamed into the phone as he leapt from his seat at the dinner table. "My niggah!"

His mother gave him a scornful look and shook her finger at him. "This is a Christian household."

"Sorry, Ma," Tony said as he walked into the living room. "Zebby, where you at, man?"

"Back in New York."

"Really, when did you get out?" Tony whispered, looking over his shoulder to see his mother eavesdropping. "Hold on a minute, man," Tony said, and walked back into the kitchen. "Ma, hang this up. I'm gonna take it on the cordless in my room."

Ethel took the phone and then said, "You don't have no manners, boy?"

"What?" Tony asked, throwing hands up in the air.

Ethel just glared at him.

"Oh, okay, *please*," Tony threw over his shoulder as he walked away. "Hey, sorry about that, Zebby. So what's good? How long you been back?"

"I been out for about a month, but I was chillin' in L.A."

"Word? Got some new honey out there?"

"Yeah, you know how it is."

They shared a few minutes of laughter before Tony said, "You ain't changed one bit."

"Well, you know, man, what can I say. So what you up to?"

"You know, same ol', same ol'. Got a new gig at Greene Investments."

"Really? Yeah, that company is doing all right for itself. I saw that third-quarter earnings exceeded the markets speculations."

Tony laughed. "They get the *Wall Street Journal* Down Under?"

"Yeah, man—you know I keep up."

"So what now?"

"What you mean?"

Tony pushed his bedroom door closed and sat down on the edge of his bed. "You going straight or what?"

"Hmmmm . . . we can talk about that when I see you. What's your schedule look like this week?"

"Um, well, I have a meeting after work tomorrow, but then I'm free."

"How about we connect on Thursday. We'll meet at the spot. You remember, don't you?"

"Yeah, man, of course."

"About seven?"

"Cool."

"Okay, man, I'm out. I'll see you then. Say hello to your moms for me, a'ight?"

"You know my moms ain't never liked you, nigger." Tony laughed and hung up the phone.

Fifteen

Mildred stood on the subway platform awaiting the number two train to come rolling through. The trains were a total mess that morning, running twenty minutes behind schedule.

When the train finally arrived, she pushed herself on with the rest of the grumbling straphangers and found herself caught in the middle of the car, pressed up against the pole in such a way that when the train jerked into motion, she experienced a small thrill down between her legs.

She yelped in surprise and embarrassment. Had she really felt that?

She wiggled her hips a bit and was awarded with another jolt of pleasure.

Mildred snickered to herself and looked around cautiously to see if any of her fellow passengers had noticed.

When they finally arrived at Franklin Avenue, the conductor announced that the train would be running on the 4 line, making express stops only. Twenty percent of the passengers groaned and stepped off, clashing with fifty percent of the people who were already waiting on the platform.

There was a small scuffle at the door between two women who looked well into their fifties. Mildred watched with awe as they shoved and cussed each other until a police officer approached and pulled them both from the car.

Mildred secured a seat and dug deep into her cloth tote bag and pulled out the latest issue of *African-American Brides*. She'd dog-eared some pages the night before and now sat drooling over the photographs.

"Congratulations."

Mildred turned and met the striking green eyes of a young woman with a pierced nose.

"Huh?"

"I said congratulations," the woman said, pointing to the glossy magazine page. "On your engagement."

Mildred continued to offer her a dumbfounded gaze.

"On your wedding!" The woman beamed.

Mildred blinked and then nodded. "Thank you."

"So do you have a date yet?"

"Um, well, we haven't decided yet," Mildred heard herself say with horror. What was she doing?

"Oh, me and my fiancé are getting married next April,

but we haven't decided on a specific date yet. I figured getting the month pinned down is half the battle."

Mildred nodded again.

"Have you started looking at reception halls yet?"

Mildred shook her head no.

"Oh my God," the woman said as she threw her head back in one dramatic motion, "it is so aggravating!"

Mildred just stared.

"But finally we've decided on the Brooklyn Opera House."

Brooklyn Opera House? Mildred had never heard of it.

"Sounds nice," Mildred said, closing the magazine and turning a bit toward the woman. "Where is it?"

"Well, it's called the Grand Prospect Hall and it's on Prospect Avenue. It's gorgeous. Gorgeous!" the woman said, throwing her hands up into the air and knocking the *New York Times* out of the hands of the man sitting beside her. "Oops, sorry." She giggled.

"Anyway, look, you've just got to go see it," she said as she dug into her Coach pocketbook, pulling out her Black-Berry.

Mildred just stared at her.

The woman hit a few buttons and then said, "Aha— here it is. The number is . . ." she started, and then looked at Mildred. "Well, aren't you going to put it in your Black-Berry?"

Mildred blushed, "Oh, no, I forgot mine at home today." Another lie. She didn't even own a BlackBerry. What was she turning into?

"Oh. Well, do you have a pen and paper?"

Mildred dug into her sack and found an old receipt and a pencil.

The woman quickly recited the number.

"Oh, this is me," she said, springing up from her seat. "My name is Beth, by the way."

"Mildred."

"Well, it was nice to meet you, Mildred, and good luck with your wedding," she said, and bounded off the train.

Mildred looked down at the number she had written there. She told herself she would toss it, but even as the thought occurred to her she knew she wouldn't, and even more, she knew that she would call Prospect Hall and make an appointment to see the space.

When she raised her eyes, she saw that she'd been so engrossed in her conversation with Beth that she had missed her Wall Street station stop—the train was pulling out of the Lexington Avenue station.

CHAPTER

Sixteen

Zebby and Tony stood at the counter at Gray's Papaya, scarfing down chili dogs. They'd spent the last hour catching up. Tony continuously teased Zebby about his newly obtained Australian accent and his referring to him and any other guy as "mate."

"Listen," Zebby said, his face suddenly becoming serious, "I wanna thank you for taking care of my place while I was gone."

"No problem," Tony said as he dragged a napkin across his lips. "It was my pleasure," he added with a wink.

"Hey"—Zebby leaned in—"I ain't gonna have any crazy bitches showing up at my place looking for you, am I?"

"Nah, man. Nah," Tony said.

"You sure?"

"Positive."

Zebby gave Tony a penetrating look before he reached into his pocket and pulled out a crumpled tissue. "I got you something. My way of saying thanks," he said as he set the tissue down on the counter.

Tony eyed it. "You shouldn't have."

"No, you deserve it."

"I hope you didn't spend too much time shopping for it." Tony's voice was heavy with sarcasm.

"Look, Negro," Zebby said, picking the tissue up and shaking it. A platinum and diamond ring fell out and onto the counter.

Tony's eyes bulged. "Damn," he said as he reached for the ring. It was heavy. Tony brought the ring to eye level. Even he, an amateur, could see the clarity of the diamonds. The ring was expensive.

"Thanks, man," Tony said as he slipped it onto his finger. Later, when he returned home, he would slip it off and place it in his jewelry box for safekeeping.

"No problem," Zebby said with a shrug. "So," he continued, slapping his hands loudly together, "now on to business."

Zebby explained that while he was in Australia he'd hooked up with a white boy who had almost bankrupted Harrods with an intensely complicated insurance scam that involved some very high-power players.

The gentleman—Zebby wouldn't divulge his name— had shared some of his most profitable scams with Zebby, one of which, coincidentally, involved inactive accounts.

Tony was half listening; he was too busy ogling the ring on his finger like a newly engaged virgin.

"Uh-huh," Tony mumbled.

"You see, man, that's where you come in."

Now Zebby had his attention. "What?"

"You. That's where you come in."

"Me?" Tony was dumbfounded. The most serious crime he'd ever committed was boosting a suit from Abraham and Strauss, and that was back in the eighties, before all of the sophisticated crime-stopper technology.

"Yeah, man. You work with dead accounts."

"Yes."

"So you can be my in guy. Of course, I'll split all the proceeds with you, fifty-fifty," Zebby said, his eyes sparkling.

Tony looked around. Already he was feeling paranoid. Just talking about it made him feel uneasy.

"I don't know, Zebby," he said, shaking his head.

"Look," Zebby said, leaning in closer. "It's real simple. All you have to do is transfer the money from the dead accounts into an active one."

Zebby made it sound so easy.

"I'll open the active accounts. I've got loads of social security numbers, addresses, names—"

Tony jumped up from the stool. He was twisting the ring around and around on his finger. He'd broken into a sweat. He could hear the cell door clanging shut.

"I can't, man. I can't do that."

He didn't want to seem like a punk, but this was his life that Zebby was trying to fuck with. They were friends, but they weren't close enough for him to put his freedom on the line.

"Nah, nah. Count me out," Tony said.

Zebby bit down hard on his bottom lip. "Sit down," he said, pointing to the empty stool. "Just hear me out."

Tony reluctantly sat down. He would listen, even though his mind was made up.

CHAPTER

Seventeen

Tony was careful to make sure that he always had the earphones to his iPod tucked into his ears whenever he entered the office building.

Over the past two weeks, he'd noticed that Mildred always seemed to be in the lobby when he arrived in the morning.

She'd jump onto the elevator with him and try to make small talk. It made him uncomfortable, the way she looked at him, her eyes so filled with . . . well, he didn't know quite what it was he was seeing in her eyes, but it made his balls tingle, which had always been a clear warning sign for him.

It took him days to realize that their morning meetings weren't happenstance but intentional.

The week before, a very suspicious Tony entered the building lobby through the bank, and his suspicions were confirmed. There was Mildred standing near the lobby elevators, checking her watch and watching the main entrance doors.

So he had started coming in through the bank regularly. That lasted all but a week before she caught on and began to position herself near the reception desk, which afforded her a bird's-eye view of all entrances.

So Tony was forced to settle on Plan B: iPod in ears and eyes on the ground.

So even though he didn't have it turned on, he pretended he did, bopping his head up and down to nothing while Mildred stood behind him chirping hello.

The elevator doors opened on the sixth floor and Tony stepped off, leaving Mildred blushing with embarrassment at the back of the elevator.

Once at his desk, he pulled the chair out and sat down. Zebby's words whirled in his mind. *Hundreds of thousands of dollars. Millions, maybe.*

Tony was nursing a headache and hadn't slept a wink. Now he rummaged through his desk drawer in search of some Tylenol.

"Long night?" Habib Habib was peering over the cubicle wall. "You look like shit."

Tony ignored him until he realized he didn't have any Tylenol. "You got any aspirin or something? My head is killing me."

"Hung over?"

You see, this was the problem with corporate America,

with fucking cubicles instead of offices with doors and locks: everybody was in your damn business.

Tony bit back a harsh response and said, "Yeah, that's it."

A few seconds later Habib Habib handed him a travel pack of Excedrin. Tony chased it with his Starbucks coffee.

◆

By noon, Tony had played and replayed Zebby's conversation in his head, and with each reel he became more and more convinced that the scam was worth it.

The only problem with the plan was that the big boss, James Henderson, would have to sign off on all account transfers, and he hadn't become a partner in the firm by not paying attention. He had a keen eye, and Tony didn't see how it was he would be able to get phony papers past him. He was a hard-nosed businessman and had always fiercely protected his investors' assets. In the end Tony threw caution to the wind and on his lunch break Tony called Zebby from a pay phone. "Look, I've been thinking—"

"Say no more. Come by after you get off work."

They spent most of the night going over the details, but time after time they ran into the same wall. James Henderson.

"There must be a way," Zebby said as he stood and stretched. "There's always a way. A loophole."

Tony leaned back into the cushions of the couch and

yawned. He was tired and was beginning to think that maybe this wasn't such a good idea, and then like a bolt of lightning it hit him and he slapped his hands together.

"What? You got something?" Zebby asked, his face eager.

"I think I found the loophole," Tony said, a large grin spreading across his face.

"Yeah, what?"

"Not what," Tony said, pulling himself to his feet and reaching for his tie. "Who."

CHAPTER

Eighteen

or me?" Mildred asked again as she looked at the large bouquet of flowers in the deliveryman's hands.

"You're Mildred Johnson, right?"

"Y-yes," Mildred responded, her voice was unsure.

"Sign here."

Mildred scribbled her name on the invoice and watched as the deliveryman exited the office.

It wasn't her birthday. Mr. Henderson always sent her flowers on her birthday, but nothing as extravagant as this. There were white roses, lilies, and some type of exotic flower Mildred had seen only in magazines. It was gorgeous!

Smiling, she ripped the cellophane away from the cardboard box and fished out the card that was attached to the side.

It read

To Mildred,
from your not-so-secret admirer . . .
Tony Landry

Mildred read the card ten times. It was unbelievable. In the time he'd been working at Greene Investments, he'd barely acknowledged her. In fact, it seemed to Mildred that he was avoiding her like the plague.

She was sure the flowers were for another Mildred Johnson in the company.

Mildred turned to her computer and with shaky hands began to do a company search. There were exactly three Mildreds in the Greene Investments employee database.

But none with the surname Johnson.

Mildred pressed her hand to her chest. Her heart was beating so fast, she was beginning to feel dizzy.

Rising from her chair, she began to pace from the desk to the window, all the while looking for an explanation as to why he would send her flowers and bumping into the same conclusion: it was a mistake.

Finally, she sat down and picked up the phone and quickly dialed his extension, which she knew by heart.

"Tony Landry, Inactive Accounts—how may I help you?"

Mildred freaked at the sound of his voice and quickly hung up the phone.

"Stop it, Mildred. You're being silly," she said aloud just as Mr. Henderson stepped into the office.

He gave her a quizzical look and then his eyes fell on the bouquet.

"Well, well, Mildred, what's the occasion?"

Mildred was so flustered, she blurted out, "I'm engaged!"

Mr. Henderson's face bloomed with surprise. "W-what?" he said as his eyes slowly went to her bare ring finger.

"Oh, that's coming soon," she said, and nervously wiggled her fingers.

Mildred wanted to curl up and die. Why had she said that? How was she allowing her fantasy life to spill into her real life? She was becoming a liar.

"Well, congratulations." Mr. Henderson came over to her, bent down, and gave her a stiff hug. "I-I didn't even know you were . . . um . . . seeing anyone."

"Thank you," Mildred said, keeping her eyes low. "It hasn't been long."

Mr. Henderson was flabbergasted. He didn't know anybody but a mother could love a face like Mildred's. Then out of nowhere a saying his Jamaican wife often used came to mind:

Every hoe has its sticka-bush.

Which, loosely translated, meant there was someone for everyone.

"Well, congratulations again, and I hope you won't

keep the wedding date as much of a secret as you did your beau," he said before going into his office.

Mildred felt her eyes begin to well with tears. She'd never, ever lied to Mr. Henderson, not even a little white lie, and now she'd gone and told a whopper!

What was wrong with her?

✦

Tony stared down at the Caller ID and smiled when he saw the name.

Mildred Johnson.

He let it ring twice before he answered it. He'd hardly spoken his name before she quickly hung up.

Tony grinned.

She was flustered. Of course she was. She was sitting there at her desk trying to figure just how a dog like her had attracted the affections of a specimen like himself.

Setting the phone back down onto the cradle, he chuckled to himself. This was going to be fun.

CHAPTER

Nineteen

He did *what?*" Seneca screamed into the phone. "Liar!"

Mildred winced. Seneca could be so cruel sometimes. Wasn't Mildred worthy of flowers?

"I don't believe you. Are you sure they were meant for you? I mean, how many Mildred Johnsons are there in the company, anyway?"

Mildred wasn't going to assist Seneca in further disgracing her by divulging that she had checked because she hadn't believed it either.

"I didn't have to check, Seneca," she said smugly before hanging up on her friend.

Mildred's heart raced every time she attempted to dial Tony's extension. When five o'clock rolled around she still hadn't mustered up the nerve, so she promised herself that she would call him first thing in the morning.

No, no: better yet she would send him an e-mail, so just in case he responded with "What the hell are you talking about? I didn't send you any damn flowers," she could reply, "Sorry, my mistake—the e-mail went to the wrong Tony Landry."

There were in fact two Anthony Landrys in the company.

She had it all worked out in her mind when she pushed the glass door open and stepped out onto the busy sidewalk. She was actually feeling good about her little plan when she looked up and saw Tony leaning against the mailbox, grinning at her.

Mildred was in so much shock that she dropped the glass vase of flowers she was clutching.

Pedestrians jumped out of the way, but at least two people were splattered. "Stupid bitch," one woman spat at her as she shook her damp white linen skirt.

"Hey, hey! It was an accident!" Tony yelled at the woman, jumping to Mildred's defense.

Mildred was standing stock-still, her expression like that of a deer seconds from being mowed down by a tractor-trailer.

Tony approached her, placed a hand on her shoulder, and asked, "Are you okay?"

Mildred flinched at his touch. For weeks she'd imagined him touching her, and now it was actually happening!

"Mildred?" Tony said as he waved his hand in front of her face.

Mildred blinked rapidly and then looked Tony square in the eyes. "Um, I'm sorry," she said pitifully, and then her eyes fell to the mess of petals, stems, and glass that lay at her feet.

"It's okay. They were just flowers. I'll send you some more tomorrow," he said as he took her hand in his. "For now, would you come to dinner with me?"

She had to be dreaming. This couldn't be real.

"Mildred?" Tony gave her hand a little jerk. "I meant dinner tonight, not next year." He laughed.

Mildred swallowed hard. "Tony, I'm not really dressed for dinner . . . I—"

"I insist," Tony said, taking a few steps away from her. "And I think you look lovely," he said, his eyes rolling over her.

✦

It wasn't anyplace fancy—at least, not in Tony's opinion—but from the look on Mildred's face, she was more than impressed.

Tony pulled the chair out for her and ordered her a glass of wine even though Mildred kept insisting that she didn't drink because alcohol went straight to her head.

That's exactly what Tony wanted.

It might help her bad looks, he thought to himself, and then remembered that that only worked on the one looking at the bad-looking person and so proceeded to order himself a double vodka tonic, easy on the tonic.

"So tell me about yourself," he said, looking deep into her bifocal-covered eyes.

Mildred daintily sipped her wine. She was so nervous, her hands were shaking. "Well," she began in a tiny voice, "I was born in Hackensack, New Jersey . . ."

An hour and another glass of wine later and halfway through her entrée of spaghetti and meatballs, she was beginning to feel a little bit at ease. Tony was witty and seemed from his penetrating questions to really be interested in her. And she liked the way he was so attentive: at one point he'd used his napkin to wipe away a drop of spaghetti sauce from her chin. That move had startled her and she found herself blushing, forgetting completely what she'd been in the midst of saying.

After dinner as they stood on the sidewalk, she swayed happily, her head swimming from the wine, as Tony hailed a cab.

"Your carriage awaits, madam," Tony said as he opened the cab door and bowed.

Mildred smiled at him as she climbed in.

"Call me when you get home so that I'll know you've arrived safely, okay?" he said and winked.

Mildred nodded her head and squirmed in the leather seat, giddy.

"Um, are you sure you don't want to share the cab?" she asked coyly.

"There's nothing I'd like more, but I need to get back to the office."

Mildred beamed. He was such a hard worker.

"Are we going or what?" the cabdriver barked from the front seat.

"Hold your horses, man. Let me say a proper good night to my girl."

My girl!!! Mildred screamed inside her head.

Tony leaned in and Mildred froze. Was he actually going to kiss her? Her mouth went dry, and the closer his lips came to her face, the harder her heart thumped. When his lips finally made contact with her cheek, she thought she was going to faint.

She was home before she'd regained her full senses and realized that Tony hadn't given the cabdriver any money. Not that it bothered her. She dreamily handed over the $22.50 and floated up to her apartment.

After lying down in bed and screaming with joy into her pillow for five whole minutes, she picked up the phone to call Seneca and rub every little detail of the evening in her face. Then she thought about what Tony had said: *Make sure you call me when you get home.*

He wanted her to call him but he hadn't given her his telephone number. A minor error on both of their parts—she hadn't given hers to him. No big deal. She dialed the office. He did say he was going back to work.

Mildred hummed happily as she listened to the phone ring. When Tony's recorded voice answered and advised that he was away from his desk and to please leave a message, Mildred told herself that he was either on the other line or in the bathroom.

She called five more times, and on the sixth try, a little

disappointed that she hadn't reached him, she finally left a message.

"H-hello, Tony, I'm just calling to let you know I arrived home safely. Um, so I had a really good time, and, well, um . . . bye."

Just as she was about to hang up, she pulled the phone to her ear and hurriedly rattled off her home number.

When she hung up, she made a mental note to buy a cell phone. She didn't have one because she'd never had a reason to. But now that she and Tony were together, she wanted him to be able to reach her whenever he needed to.

Mildred giggled at the word *together*. She had never been "together" with anyone in her life!

Mildred fell back into the bed and screamed into the pillow for another ten minutes. She'd never been happier.

Then she lay there staring at the clock, waiting for Tony to call and tell her he'd received her message.

She was still waiting when her alarm went off at six o'clock the following morning.

Twenty

So what's going on? You making any headway?"
Zebby had called a meeting at Gray's Papaya.

Tony nodded his head before biting down into his chili dog. "Yeah, she's falling and fast. I sent her flowers, which by the way cost me an arm and a leg, and then I took her out to dinner. And you know what?"

"What?"

"The next day I got to work and she had sent me flowers!"

Zebby laughed as he wiped the mustard from his bushy mustache.

"It's not funny, man. I think the chick is a little psycho."

"Why do you say that?"

"I don't know, man. I'm just getting this feeling, you know?"

"A feeling?"

"Yeah, man," Tony started, and then dropped his voice an octave and leaned in closer to Zebby. "When a bitch ain't right, my balls start to tingle."

Zebby's eyes widened. "You're fucking with me, right?"

"Nah, man, I'm serious, and this chick got them tingling like a motherfucker!"

Zebby put his hand over his mouth and let out a long, hearty laugh.

"Stop laughing, man—it ain't funny."

"Yes it is!" Zebby said, and slammed his hand down on the counter. "Okay, so you got tingling balls. Maybe she's turning you on?"

Tony made a face. "Zebby," he said, his face now serene, "do I look like a bulldog?"

"What? No."

"Do I look like someone's mother?"

"Well, a motherfu—"

"I said, do I look like someone's mother?"

"Nah, why?"

"'Cause, man, only a mother or a bulldog could love a face like hers!"

"C'mon, man—it's like that?"

"Bow-fucking-wow."

"Damn."

"Yeah. Maybe you should be the one romancing her and not me."

"Nah, man, you already in. When are you going to nail her?"

Tony shivered in disgust. "Are you deaf? Did you not hear me say she was a dog? I ain't screwing her!"

Zebby laughed. "I think this is a first. Tony Landry actually turning down pussy!"

"Well, there's a first time for everything."

"So there is, my friend, so there is."

Zebby drained the rest of his Pepsi from the bottle, belched, and then said, "How much longer before you get the password?"

"I don't know, man. It's only been three days. Give me at least a week."

CHAPTER

Twenty-one

It had been a grueling three weeks.

He'd been putting in a lot of overtime at the office simply because he needed time to research the accounts that he and Zebby planned on raiding.

Habib Habib was impressed with Tony's dedication and half joked with him about the possibility that Tony was coming after his job. Tony had assured him that he was trying to do no such thing. And that was the God's honest truth.

With all of that, he also had to court Mildred. Most of their conversations took place over the phone, although they had met for lunch twice at some out-of-the-way eatery where Tony was sure he wouldn't be liable to run into anyone he knew.

So far he had been able to persuade Mildred to keep their romance a secret.

"I don't like people up in my business," he told her. "This is very special to me, and I hope you feel the same way."

Mildred did feel the same way and so agreed to keep her mouth shut. Even though she was bursting at the seams with joy.

Now his cell phone was vibrating. He didn't even have to look at the screen. He knew it was Mildred.

Taking a deep breath, he fixed his face with a smile, flipped the phone open, and said, "Hey!"

Sweetness, the spicy, green-eyed Latina bartender whose tits were practically spilling out of her red and white striped bustier, winked at him and started toward another customer.

They'd been flirting recklessly with each other since he'd walked into the bar.

"I'll come back, sweetie," she purred, before sashaying away to a waiting customer. Tony peeked over the bar to snatch a glance at her apple-shaped behind and found himself licking his lips hungrily. He wouldn't mind taking a bite out of that.

"Hi," Mildred sang back. "I just wanted to say good night, pleasant dreams, and don't let the bedbugs bite."

Tony rolled his eyes. "Right back at ya."

The bartender was coming his way again. He had to get rid of Mildred, and fast.

"Listen, sweetie, I'm here with some of the guys from the office and I don't want to be rude. Can I call—"

"Oh no, no, go ahead. I'm so sorry I interrupted you."

"But we're on for tomorrow night, right?"

"Yes. Of course. I can't wait."

"Okay, then. See you tomorrow. Have a good night."

"Okay. You have a good night too," Mildred said.

Tony flipped the Razr closed just as the bartender approached. "So, now, where were we?"

Sweetness licked her plump lips, rested ten long fingers on the bar, and gave him a seductive nod.

Tony could feel his penis begin to stiffen. This was the sexiest woman he'd come across in a long time.

"So, 'Sweetness' is actually on your birth certificate?"

"Yes it is, sugar," Sweetness responded.

Later on, Tony found himself sitting on Sweetness's black leather couch in her one-bedroom Chelsea apartment. The space was small but homey.

Sweetness had told him to help himself to the bottle of Rémy Martin on the kitchen table while she went in the bedroom to change into something a little more comfortable.

When she reemerged she was dressed in a red scalloplaced negligee that hid nothing at all.

"Well, isn't that special?" Tony heard himself say.

Sweetness walked over to the bookshelf that held everything but books and flipped on the Bose radio. The room was ignited with the erratic sounds of heavy metal. Not really Tony's bag, but hey . . . whatever, right?

Sweetness pulled a joint from behind her ear and started toward him.

"Do you indulge?" she queried, situating herself next to him.

Tony hadn't smoked a joint in more than a year. He was tempted but was still on probation at Greene Investments and could be called out for a piss test at any time, so he declined.

"But please, knock yourself out," he told Sweetness.

And she did, puffing more than half of the two-inch-long joint.

Tony in the meantime had begun to slowly undo the satin ribbons on the front of the negligee. The lace was obstructing his view, and he wanted to see those tits up close and personal.

Sweetness didn't seem to care that he was slowly undressing her. She closed her eyes and allowed her head to fall back onto the couch.

Her breasts exposed, Tony began to slowly massage them, taking one nipple and then the next into his hot mouth, sucking hungrily until Sweetness moaned with excitement.

Tony stood, pulled her to her feet, and helped her step out of the outfit. She stood before him, long, lean, and as bald as the day she was born down between her legs.

That excited him.

Pushing her gently back down onto the couch, he began to undress.

Maybe if the music weren't so loud he would have heard the key being shoved into the lock. But the music was loud, and when he finally realized what was happening, the door was open and he was naked, his dick at a full alert.

Tony had been in some precarious situations in the

past. He'd jumped out of second-floor windows, hid in closets, even spent the night under a king-size bed due to a husband returning from a business trip a day early.

So when the door swung open, he instinctively ran across the room toward the window, even though he was on the fifth floor.

Sweetness broke out in uproarious laughter. "Baby, I told you that I was single and I meant it. That's just my sister."

Tony swung around, his hand protectively shielding his now limp penis.

"What?"

"Yeah—sister. My twin sister," Sweetness said, pointing at the carbon copy likeness of her. "Hey, girl," Sweetness called to the woman, who was grinning slyly in Tony's direction. "This is Tony. Tony, this is my sister, Honey."

Tony almost laughed. "Honey?"

"Yeah," Sweetness said, reaching for the remainder of the joint and lighting it. "Our parents had a wicked sense of humor."

"Pleasure," Honey said, walking over and reaching for the joint. After two tokes, she said, "Am I interrupting something?"

"Nope." Sweetness yawned. "We were actually waiting for you."

This was news to Tony.

"Weren't we, Tony?"

Tony's face broke into a broad smile. His dick was getting hard again. "Yeah."

Honey's eyes slowly rolled over Tony's body, stopping only to ogle his member, which seemed to be reaching out to her. "Nice," she cooed as she began to roll the wintergreen tube top up and over her head, revealing two firm breasts.

"Tony," Honey said, giving him a seductive nod, "do you think you can handle both of us?"

Tony felt like he'd died and gone to heaven.

"I don't see why not," he said as he grabbed hold of his penis and wagged it at her. "The question is," he said, using his slickest tone, "can you two handle me?"

The girls exchanged knowing looks.

Tony followed the twins into the bedroom. The largest bed he'd ever seen floated in the middle of the scarlet-colored bedroom. Scented candles glowed from all corners of the room, and Tony looked up and was pleasantly surprised to see a large mirror on the ceiling above the bed.

Honey took him by the hand and gently guided him onto the bed, where she began to plant warm kisses on his lips and neck. Sweetness walked out of view, into one of the two walk-in closets. When she returned, she had a long, thick, chocolate-colored dildo in her hands.

Sweetness pushed Tony gently down onto his back and took his engorged penis into her mouth. Honey crawled into bed and kissed Tony passionately before climbing onto his chest. Her vagina was just millimeters away from his face. "I know what you want," he moaned as Sweetness twirled her tongue around the tip of his penis.

Tony grabbed hold of Honey's hips and pulled her forward until he was able to close his mouth over her cunt.

They came seconds apart, Honey hitting a high note and slapping her hands against the wooden headboard, while Tony's legs went rigid and his eyes rolled up into his skull.

The three lay there for a long moment, panting and cuddling. After a while, Sweetness rose from the bed and walked off to the bathroom. Tony could hear water running and imagined she was rinsing her mouth clean of his juices. Honey climbed off him and reached into the nightstand, from where she pulled an extra-large Magnum condom.

Tony stared up at himself in the mirror and wasn't at all surprised to see that his penis was still erect.

These twins, he thought to himself, really have a way with their mouths. Before he knew it, Honey had used hers to roll the condom onto his member.

"My turn," Sweetness cooed as she strutted back into the bedroom and mounted Tony. She eased herself down onto his stiffness and began to slowly ride him. Tony gripped her buttocks. The pleasure was intense—she was as tight as a virgin.

Meanwhile, Honey splayed herself out alongside of them, watching them intensely as she slowly inserted the dildo between her legs, keeping time with her sister's rhythm.

Five minutes later, the three were howling with mounting excitement and Tony was on his way to the second of four explosive orgasms he would have that night.

CHAPTER

Twenty-two

Mildred couldn't hold it any longer. She knew she'd promised Tony that their secret was safe with her, but she was bursting for someone else to know, and so she found herself spilling her guts to Seneca.

Seneca's mouth hung open in shock.

"And if you call me a liar, I'll never speak to you again."

Seneca blinked and then said, "Proof."

Mildred was ready for this one, and so she pulled her cell phone from her purse, flipped it open, and then began to scroll through the pictures she'd snapped.

Seneca's mouth was open again. "When the hell did you get a cell phone?"

"A few days ago," Mildred responded casually. "Here," she said, passing the phone over to Seneca.

There on the tiny screen was a picture of her and Tony, hand in hand in the Financial District in front of the famed bronze bull statue.

"You'll catch flies if you don't close your mouth," Mildred warned.

"When was this taken?"

"Yesterday. We went to lunch."

Seneca gave her a suspicious look. "Who took it?"

"Some Japanese tourist," Mildred said, taking the phone from Seneca's hands and gazing lovingly at the picture.

Seneca shook her head in disbelief.

"What?" Mildred said.

"Nothing, girl. I'm just kind of dumbfounded, that's all."

Mildred's feelings were immediately wounded, and her expression showed it.

"No, no, not that I'm saying you don't deserve it," Seneca said, throwing her hands up in defense. "I'm just saying that it's rare that you go from never ever having someone to . . . to . . . that!" Seneca snatched the phone from Mildred's hands in order to get another look. "So how is he?"

"He's fine," Mildred responded, practically prying the phone from Seneca's hands.

"No, I mean . . . *how is he?*"

Mildred didn't quite get where she was coming from, and then she saw the sly look on Seneca's face.

"Oh."

"Well?"

"We, um . . . I . . ."

"You haven't fucked him yet?"

Mildred blushed. There was nothing more she wanted to do, considering she'd never done it. Well, at least not with another person.

"No, we haven't."

Actually, one evening over the phone she'd suggested, rather meekly, that Tony come by to spend the night. She remembered how her heart had dropped down into her stomach when he didn't immediately respond. The silence seemed to have gone on forever when finally his voice came back and he said, "Mildred, you are very special to me. I don't want to mess this up by having sex with you too soon. You mean much more to me than that."

She couldn't tell Seneca that. In her mind sex was the end all be all, and besides, she would just find some way to turn his statement around and against her. And God forbid Mildred own up to the fact that they hadn't even kissed. At least, not on the lips.

So Mildred raised her head and announced ever so proudly. "I thought it best we wait."

Seneca's eyes went wide. "Wait? What are you waiting for—marriage?"

"Maybe."

"Now I know you've lost your fucking mind. Do you think a man that looks like that is going to—"

Seneca caught herself. There was no way in the world that a fine-looking brother like that was going to marry Mildred. True, Mildred was her friend, and maybe there was somebody out in the world that might want her for his wife. But not Tony. She didn't know what he was doing with Mildred, but none of it seemed kosher.

"Going to what, Seneca?" Mildred's eyes glowed with anger.

Seneca cleared her throat. "Do you think a man like that is going to wait forever, Mildred?"

CHAPTER

Twenty-three

Tony had taken Mildred out exactly eight times.

Four dinners, three lunches, and one brunch.

He'd been in her apartment twice. Each time she'd prepared a meal fit for a king. That was the one good thing about her. She could cook her ass off!

Tony always arrived with wine, hoping he could get drunk enough to accomplish the unthinkable.

Sex.

But it never happened. He couldn't even bring himself to kiss her. He thought those jutting front teeth might shear his tongue right off.

Mildred seemed happy enough just to have him there, meeting him at the door with a pair of brown suede slippers she'd bought specially for him. She prepared his plate and even tried to hand-feed him once, but he gently refused the assistance.

From the way she fawned over him and fulfilled his every request, he supposed that if he retired to the bathroom to take a shit and then called to her to come wipe his ass, she would be more than happy to oblige him in that area as well.

Zebby was pressuring him, pushing him to wrap things up. And by wrapping things up, he meant fucking her.

"I'm going out of town for a few days, so you can bring her here. I don't care if you have to drink a whole bottle of Hennessey and put a paper bag over her head, you do what you gotta do to make your man work. I'll even leave some *Playboy*s and some string in the john to help you out—"

"String?" Tony had asked, confused.

"Yeah, man—you get your shit hard and tie it off at the base, it'll block the blood from draining out and you'll stay stiff. Or if you like I can get you some Viagra . . ."

Neither option interested Tony. He would just have to close his eyes and think of the twins, Sweetness and Honey.

✦

Mildred stood in front of the small bathroom mirror critiquing her outfit. She didn't own any real going-out clothes. All of her outfits were either for work—matronly skirt suits and dresses—or weekend wear, jeans and T-shirts. Luckily their dinner dates had all occurred after work. But tonight was Saturday and she had no idea where they were going, but she was pretty sure that what hung in her closet would not be appropriate.

She made a face and straightened the Peter Pan collar of the white blouse she wore. It used to be her favorite blouse, but now it seemed childish and old-fashioned. She'd paired the top with a light gray pinstripe skirt and her black leather rubber-soled work shoes.

"I look horrible!" she screamed at her reflection.

Just as she made up her mind to rummage through the closet and find something else to wear, the doorbell rang.

She ran to the intercom, pressed the button, and uttered a breathless "Who?"

"It's Tony. Come down."

Too late to make any changes now, she thought as she snatched up her pocketbook and rushed out of the apartment.

✦

It was the first time she'd ever been in his car. It was luxurious, a silver Lexus coup with black leather interior.

"This is nice," Mildred said as she moved her palm over the leather seat.

"Thanks," Tony said without looking at her.

Soft jazz poured out of the speakers as they sped down Sullivan Place toward Bedford Avenue. Tony seemed to be distracted, and Mildred began to wonder if she had done something wrong. If maybe her outfit had offended him.

"So," he said suddenly, startling Mildred, "I was thinking that tonight I'd cook dinner for you at my place." He still wasn't looking at her—his eyes remained focused on the road.

"Really!" Mildred squealed. She was bursting with happiness; she couldn't believe this was happening to her. The past three weeks had seemed like a fantasy. Every morning she woke up believing that the previous day was just a dream. And she braced herself each and every time she sat down at her desk and picked up the phone to dial Tony's extension. She always expected to hear his prepackaged greeting—because if she heard that it would confirm that everything she'd thought had happened hadn't.

But every morning it was the same: "Good morning, beautiful. How are you?"

So now, sitting in that car, speeding along toward Tony's apartment, she wrapped her arms around herself and carefully grabbed hold of the fleshy part of her upper arms and pinched until her eyes watered.

Yep, this was really happening.

✦

When they pulled up in front of the apartment building, Mildred thought that maybe they were just making a stop. She had all of Tony's personal info memorized, and so when he backed the car into a space in front of the building on Vanderbilt Avenue, bells went off in her head warning her that it wasn't the address he'd listed on his application form.

There had to be a perfectly logical explanation, and she was sure that before the evening was over he would provide one.

The apartment was beautiful, like something out of *Metropolitan Home*. The coffee table, which was a large leather ottoman, had already been set for dinner, complete with linen napkins and candles.

"Please sit down," Tony said, taking her by the hand and guiding her to the sofa.

"Gosh, Tony." Mildred sighed. "This is beautiful."

"Beautiful women deserve beautiful things," Tony said, and then forced the bile back down into his stomach. "I hope you like Japanese?"

"Oh, I do!"

"Good," Tony said, rubbing his hands together. "I prepped the food before I came to get you, so it'll only take a minute." He turned around and walked into the kitchen. "A mahimahi and avocado roll, stir-fried vegetables over buckwheat soba noodles, and ginger-glazed chicken breast," he yelled from the kitchen.

Mildred was nervous; her hands were beginning to sweat.

"Champagne?" Tony called from the kitchen.

"Y-yes, thank you," Mildred said.

When Tony walked into the room with a flute filled with bubbly, Mildred looked at him expectantly.

"Here you go," he said, handing her the flute.

"Thank you."

Tony hit the switch on the Bose entertainment center and walked away. Again, smooth jazz filled her ears. Mildred sat and sipped her champagne, realizing much too late that the drink was adding to the furnace raging inside of her.

She would be drunk in a minute.

"Tony?"

"Yeah?"

"Where's the, um . . . ladies' room?"

Tony poked his head around the doorway of the kitchen. "Right down the hall and to your left."

The bathroom was made up of shiny black and white tiles. It was pristine, and Mildred felt bad about using the bright white hand towel to dry her hands.

When she was done, she was horrified to see that the hand cream she'd used had left long yellow streaks on the towel.

She spun around and around, looking for a place to stash the evidence. Where was the hamper? Finally, she balled up the towel and stuffed it behind the toilet bowl.

She was about to reach for the doorknob when curiosity got the best of her and she swung the mirrored door of the medicine cabinet open. Stacked inside were boxes and boxes of Trojans.

"Oh my goodness," Mildred muttered to herself as she slammed the door closed again.

"Hey, hey, you okay in there?" Tony's voice came from the other side of the door.

"Y-yes. I'll be right out."

✦

During dinner all Mildred could think about were those endless boxes of condoms. Who needed so many? She found her eyes drifting down to Tony's pants and the ever-present bulge there. She wondered how many vaginas his penis had entered and if it would ever find its way into hers.

"Mildred? Mildred?" Tony was snapping his fingers in her face yet again. "You drift off a lot, huh?"

Mildred nodded. "Yes, it's a bad habit, I guess."

After dinner Mildred practically begged Tony to allow her to wash the dishes, but he wouldn't have it. He said, "That's why I have Amana."

"Amana? Is that your maid?"

Tony roared with laughter, and after wiping the tears from his eyes he said, "No, that's the dishwasher. The dishwasher is made by Amana."

Mildred felt ridiculous. "Oh, yes, of course. Ha-ha," she said, blushing with embarrassment.

She assumed they'd gone through an entire bottle of champagne, because she felt as light as a feather and giddy. Tony had dimmed the overhead lights and now the room glowed with candlelight.

Looking over at Tony, she saw that he seemed engrossed in the music, his head swaying from side to side as he tapped his foot along with the melody.

Mildred's eyes grew heavy and her head fell back onto the couch. She started to dream and then jolted awake when she heard herself begin to snore.

That's when she realized that Tony's hand was on her knee.

"What—where—" Her head snapped up.

"Relax, Mildred," Tony whispered as he gently patted her knee.

Mildred was trying to relax, but her body wouldn't listen. It had gone as stiff as a corpse.

Tony leaned in close and kissed her cheek and then her jaw line, and then before she knew it her earlobe was in his mouth; all the while his hand was slowly stroking her thigh.

"Relax," he said again, and with that he used his free hand to turn her face toward his.

Inside she was screaming, This is it! This is it! It's finally going to happen!

She quickly became wet with desire. It was as if some internal faucet had suddenly been turned on.

Squeezing her knees tightly together, she took a few shuddering breaths and forced herself to remain calm.

Tony inhaled deeply and diverted his eyes as he leaned in to kiss her. It was as he had imagined it. His lips made direct contact with her protruding teeth.

Mildred mumbled an apology.

Tony sighed; he didn't know how he was going to get through it.

Enough kissing, he thought as he gently removed her glasses and then slowly began to undo the top button of her blouse.

Mildred, her eyelids fluttering and mouth still open,

watched anxiously as Tony undid first one button, then a second, then a third . . .

Tony wanted to tell her to close her mouth, that that part of tonight's activities was over.

Her blouse unbuttoned, he almost jumped up and walked right out of that apartment. It was going to take him half the night to peel her out of the mess of spandex and rubber Mildred called a girdle.

Mildred couldn't see much without her glasses on. All she knew was that he had suddenly stopped.

"What's wrong?"

The sound of her voice snapped Tony back to life. "It's just that . . ." he trailed off, and then switched gears. "Mildred, I want to make love to you."

Mildred's breath caught in her throat.

"Do you want to make love to me, Mildred?"

"Oh, yes, Tony. Yes, I do," she squealed, suddenly overwhelmed with emotion. Catching him off-guard, she grabbed his face between her two meaty hands. Before Tony knew it, Mildred's tongue was in his mouth, lapping away at his palate as if it were a bowl of milk.

Gagging, he finally pulled his face away and resisted the urge to wipe his hand across his mouth.

"Let's . . . let's go to the bedroom," Tony said.

To save time, Tony suggested she prepare herself for him while he went to the bathroom and did the same.

Mildred's mind wandered again to the boxes of condoms. They would have to talk about that. Now that he had her, he wouldn't need anyone else.

In the darkness of the room Mildred quickly stripped

down to nothing and climbed into the bed. Pulling the covers up to her chin, she waited, her heart racing.

Tony stood in front of the mirror. His hands gripped the porcelain edge of the sink as he stared his reflection directly in the eye.

"What are you about to do? Are you really going to do this? You know doing this is the equivalent of selling your soul to the devil, don't you? And all for what? Some money? Is that who you are?"

Tony stared at himself a little bit more before he sat down on the toilet and flipped open one of the magazines Zebby had left underneath the cabinet for him.

He flipped through page after page as he stroked himself erect. When he was as hard as he thought he could possibly become, he went to her.

He'd barely climbed in before she was on her side, her hands like octopus limbs all over his body, exploring every inch of him and then finally grabbing hold of his dick.

He'd never in all of his years of fucking felt as though he was the one being taken advantage of.

"Oh, oh," Mildred mumbled as she stroked his Johnson. Her hands were surprisingly soft, and Tony had to admit, he was experiencing some pleasure from her touch.

"Oh, Tony, oh," Mildred moaned as she stroked him. "I've dreamed of this moment for so long," she said breathlessly as she released his penis and slid her hand across his abdomen and then up his side before settling on his bicep and kneading the skin there.

Tony had no desire to caress her—that slight interest had been shattered when he'd reached out and his hand fell on her fleshy gut. His hand had immediately recoiled and now lay lifeless on the two inches of bedsheet that separated them.

"Me too," he managed as his hard-on began to die.

Desperate to regain some momentum, he moved his hand up to her breasts, which were large and long. At his touch, Mildred began to tremble and moan. She grabbed her left breast and shoved it toward his mouth.

He obliged, surprised to find that her nipples were almost as long as his pinky fingers.

"Oh God, oh God," Mildred cried out when he began to suck. "Yes, baby, yes."

Tony felt his jimmy jump. He was actually getting off on the pleasure he was giving her.

Suddenly, Mildred flipped violently onto her back. "Take me, take me now!" she wailed.

Tony uttered a little prayer, tore the package of the condom he'd been clutching in his free hand, and rolled the rubber over his dick.

He mounted her and Mildred braced herself.

Tony situated the tip of his penis at the opening of her vagina, took a deep breath, and slowly began to thrust himself in.

An animal-like sound escaped from Mildred, and her body began to shake.

"Are you okay?" Tony whispered breathlessly into her ear.

Her only response was a quick nod.

Tony planted his hands on either side of Mildred, bracing himself on his arms, and proceeded to push himself deeper into her.

When he was halfway in, Mildred began to gasp for air; he didn't bother to ask if he should continue because her hands had a steel grip on his waist, pulling him deeper.

When he was all the way in, he began to thrust harder, faster.

Mildred was screaming his name, crying out in a mixture of pain and pleasure.

"You like it, you like it?"

"Y-yes!" Mildred responded in a hoarse whisper.

Sex scenes from the blue movies she'd watched over the years flashed through her mind, and she courageously raised her legs and wrapped them around Tony's back, hooking her ankles together and pinning him down on top of her.

"Ugh," Tony managed before his air supply was completely blocked off. Mildred, still happily thrusting, took a while to notice that Tony had stopped moving.

"Tony? Tony?"

Mildred removed her head from the space between his neck and shoulder and turned to look Tony in the face. In the darkness of the room she could see the whites of his eyes.

"Tony?" She called again, finally unlocking her legs.

"D-don't ever do that again," he gasped.

"Oh, sorry," Mildred mumbled, a bit embarrassed.

Tony began to move again, long, even strokes that Mildred received with small, excited grunts of pleasure. Lost in the sweetness of the moment, she began to roll her hips against his. Tony groaned with delight and he began to grind in time with Mildred. He smiled in spite of his earlier misgivings and thought as he gripped Mildred's shoulders and pushed himself deeper that this wasn't bad, not bad at all.

Twenty-four

Sunday had come and gone, and by Monday Mildred found she still couldn't pull herself together.

"Is everything okay, Mildred?" Mr. Henderson asked, genuine concern in his voice. Mildred had never once called in sick.

"I think I might be catching the flu," Mildred lied in a nasal voice.

"Oh, my. Well, you take care of yourself. I'll have Amy cover for you."

"Thank you, Mr. Henderson. I'm sure I'll be well enough to come in tomorrow."

Mildred hung up the phone.

She kept replaying his words in her head as he was

pushing up into her: *Oh, you're so tight, you're so fucking sweet, Jesus Christ,* he'd moaned into her neck.

It had hurt like hell, and she'd had no idea how she was supposed to move her body or even *if* she was supposed to move her body. She'd seen plenty of porno films, but those people were actors. Expert actors. She was a novice, but she would learn and she would become just as good as the people who starred in those blue movies.

She felt a snap deep down inside of her, and she thought Tony had felt it too, because he'd paused in mid-thrust and stared into the darkness over her head, and then he'd pushed himself so deep into her that she thought he would break through her back. She'd screamed while his body shook so violently she thought he was having an epileptic attack.

Afterward, Tony's loud snores cut through the night as Mildred lay on her side, staring at Tony's muscled back.

He hadn't held her; in fact, he'd scurried over to the edge of the bed, leaving her shivering in the wet spot.

CHAPTER

Twenty-five

A virgin?"

"Can you believe it? In this day and age?" Tony laughed.

Errol shook his head in disgust. His friend had dropped down to a level that Errol had not known even existed.

"Why are you even messing with that woman, Tony? She's not even your type. You yourself said she was a dog."

"Hey, you know how it is . . ." Tony said, trailing off. He couldn't tell Errol what he was up to. Errol was his boy, but he was straight-laced and would never agree to what Tony was planning. At the very least, he'd try to talk him out of it. But he might just report him.

"I guess it's true what my mother always said," Errol said as he went up for the rebound.

"What was that?" Tony asked as he caught the ball and did a quick spin, jumped up, and dunked the ball.

"Dick don't have no conscience."

◆

Maybe his dick didn't have a conscience, but Tony believed that he did, even though the thought of money beat it back every time. But if he had to tell the truth, it would be this: As soon as he felt more than heard Mildred's hymen give way, he knew he was going to be in a world of trouble. It was nice to be someone's first when you were a teenager or in your early twenties, but in your thirties, you've lived some and learned some and any sexually educated man knew that being with a virgin was fleeting pleasure, because what that woman expected from you beyond that night was nothing less than your entire being.

Tony needed to have a few days to himself. A few days to prepare for the onslaught of affection, admiration, and those three little words that he could already feel dangling above him like a hangman's noose: *I love you.*

So he told her he was going out of town to take care of some business and wouldn't return until Tuesday morning, just in time for work. He explained that where he was going, up in the Catskills, the cell phone service was sketchy and that he would be sure to call her once he got back into town.

It was as if he'd never even made that statement, because it was Sunday afternoon and she'd already sent him twenty-two text messages.

CHAPTER

Twenty-six

Seneca was quiet on the other end of the phone. For a minute, Mildred thought the line had gone dead, until she heard Seneca exhale and then say, "You did not!"

"I did," Mildred said calmly.

"Was it good?"

Mildred didn't quite understand the question. It'd hurt like hell and there was none of the cuddling she'd hoped for. After an hour Tony had jumped up suddenly and announced that he had to take her home because he was driving upstate to handle some business. They'd driven in silence and once again she thought she'd done something wrong, and when she voiced that, he quickly calmed her fears by taking her hand, bringing it to his lips and kissing it, and then saying, "How could you ask me something like that? This was the most perfect night of my life."

"Yes," Mildred breathed into the phone, "it was more than good. It was the most perfect night of my life."

✦

The following day, as Mildred stood waiting for the train to arrive, she wondered if people could see the difference in her. She wondered if she had a different walk. If she had that devirginized glow about her. She certainly felt different.

"Glad to have you back, Mildred," Mr. Henderson said when he walked in Tuesday morning and saw Mildred at her desk, already busy at work. "Are you feeling better? You're certainly looking well."

"Oh, yes. I'm much better." Mildred beamed. "It must have been one of those twenty-four-hour viruses."

Mr. Henderson gave Mildred a skeptical look. "Must have been," he said as he picked up the *Wall Street Journal* from her desk and walked to his office.

✦

Later at lunch, as Geneva looked thoughtfully at her tuna fish on whole wheat sandwich and then back at Mildred, she could see the glow. She didn't know if it had anything to do with having sex for the first time. She did know that that glow usually accompanied extreme happiness. But she felt that this happiness Mildred was experiencing was fleeting, and so she wanted to choose her words very carefully.

She liked Mildred and thought she was a truly wonderful person, but she also believed that Mildred was naive.

"You have to be careful with your heart," Geneva said. "I mean, from what you're telling me, this is your first love—not counting Michael Jackson, of course." Geneva giggled.

Geneva wanted to keep it light. She certainly didn't want Mildred to think that she was judging or attacking her in any way. Because she too had been there: the overweight, underconfident woman suddenly being pursued by a man so fine, Geneva had thought his good looks was just his cover for crazy.

But he'd been genuine, and now they were husband and wife.

So who was she to tell Mildred that this thing she'd suddenly stumbled onto wasn't real, even though deep down in Geneva's heart the whole situation just didn't feel right?

"I will," Mildred said, and patted Geneva on the arm.

Geneva forced a smile. It was the happiest she'd ever seen Mildred. She would let her have her moment, but she'd be keeping a close watch on the situation.

CHAPTER

Twenty-seven

That Saturday, Tony and Mildred were in Prospect Park. The main field, surrounded by trees, gave the illusion of being miles away from any concrete structure.

He'd really outdone himself with this one.

He had a red and white checkered blanket and a picnic basket filled with gourmet snacks, complete with a bottle of champagne and an ounce of caviar—that little tidbit had been a gift from Zebby. Tony would never have spent that type of money on any woman.

All around them lovers were splayed out on blankets. Single women sunned their bikini-clad upper torsos while bopping their heads to the music that streamed out of their iPods. Shirtless men tossed Frisbees to one another and their dogs.

"It's really a beautiful day, isn't it?" Tony said as he spooned the caviar onto toast points.

Mildred had never had caviar, although it had always been part of her daydreams.

"Open up," Tony said as he glided the salty treat toward her mouth. Mildred opened her mouth to receive it the same way she'd done with his cock the other night.

She'd spent the past three days reviewing porno movie after porno movie, taking pages and pages of notes.

Seneca had counseled her on the art of the blow job, acting it out on a skinned banana. "It's important not to let your teeth get in the way. They don't like that," she'd advised.

And so that evening when Tony came to visit, she guided him to the couch, undid his pants, and began to do to him what she'd done to two pounds of Chiquita bananas.

She didn't like it, not one bit, but Tony seemed to love it, his face full of ecstasy and his head swinging from side to side.

"A gentleman won't come in your mouth. He'll pull out before he comes," Seneca had warned.

Mildred didn't quite believe that statement, because even though Tony had held tight to her head and pushed his dick deep down into her throat, coating her tonsils with semen, she still believed him to be a gentleman and the best thing that had ever happened to her.

Now the caviar on her tongue pulled her back to that night and she fought the urge to gag.

"Do you like it?"

Mildred shrugged her shoulders and then spat it out into her napkin when Tony looked away.

After the meal and a glass of champagne, Tony stretched himself out across the blanket and rested his head in her lap. She marveled at his deep brown skin, which seemed to shimmer in the sunlight. He was dressed in a sleeveless white Nike T-shirt and a pair of gray sweatpants.

Mildred had donned a pair of high-water jeans that were faded at the knees. Those and a pink terry-cloth top that she'd bought at Conways the previous summer.

"Touch me," he said, and took her hand and placed it on his cheek. "I like it when you touch me."

Mildred blushed. He was always saying things like that. She looked deep into his eyes and began stroking his cheek. Tony held her eyes with his and a small, satisfied smile appeared on his lips.

"I want to tell you something, Mildred Johnson," he said, his voice taking on a serious tone.

Mildred felt her breath catch in her throat, and her hand slowed to a stop.

"No, don't stop," Tony said. "It feels good."

Mildred's hand sprang into motion again.

"What I want to tell you is," Tony started, and then took in a great gulp of air. He was going to be nominated for an Academy fucking Award for this particular performance, he told himself as he forced his eyes to fill with tears.

"I want to tell you that even though we've only been together a short time . . . I think I might be . . ."

Mildred held her breath. Surely he wasn't going to say what she'd been waiting to hear her entire life? It couldn't be.

". . . falling in love with you."

Mildred was blinking. Blinking back her tears of joy. But still she needed to hear it again. She needed to make sure he was using that word, that magical word: *love*.

Tony pulled himself up and took Mildred's face into his hands. Their noses were less than an inch apart, and when he spoke, she could feel his warm breath against her face. "No, no, I was wrong . . ."

Mildred's heart sank.

"I was holding back," Tony said. "I don't think I'm falling in love with you. I'm already in love with you. I love you," Tony said, and then planted a passionate kiss on Mildred's lips.

Mildred's body shook in his arms, and when their lips parted, she heard herself say, "I love you too."

Tony's eyes widened. "You do?" he said, as if not believing. "You love me?"

Mildred wrapped her arms around his neck. "I do, I do—I love you." She repeated her words over and over again as she bounced up and down on the blanket.

Later, as they strolled hand in hand toward the exit, Tony stopped every person that came within a foot of them to say, "Hey, she loves me. Mildred Johnson loves *meeeeeeeee!*"

CHAPTER

Twenty-eight

Mildred had never in life cashed a check for more than sixty dollars, but there she was, staring at the smiling teller behind the glass shield at Chase Manhattan Bank as he counted and then recounted the ten one-hundred-dollar bills.

"Thank you, Ms. Johnson, and have a nice day," the woman said as she slid the money into the silver tray.

Mildred was going shopping. She was going to buy herself a few new outfits, as well as a gift or two for Tony.

She wasn't a savvy shopper. She didn't know anything about the high-end retail stores—she had always purchased her clothes at Sears and JCPenney—but now she found herself walking down Fulton Street headed straight to Macy's.

It was Saturday morning and the store was buzzing with shoppers. Mildred immediately felt overwhelmed.

Geneva had promised to meet her in the women's section at ten-thirty. Mildred needed help with her wardrobe and she hadn't asked Seneca because she felt that Seneca's choice in clothing was a bit too sleazy.

Geneva, on the other hand, while older, seemed to have a knack when it came to dressing her plus-size body.

"Hey, girl!" Geneva squealed as Mildred stepped off the escalator.

They hugged each other.

"Well, first off, we have to get you into something other than gray, black, and brown, okay?"

Mildred nodded. "I'm all yours."

The women's section, in Geneva's opinion, didn't hold much of a variety. "We should have gone to the Thirty-fourth Street store—they would have had more to choose from. But we can always check out Lane Bryant as well, if we don't find anything in here," Geneva grumbled as she flipped through the carousel racks of clothes.

In the end, they decided on three brightly colored summer dresses, two pairs of pedal pushers—one in a washed-out denim and another in khaki—and two baby-doll tops that took the emphasis away from Mildred's midsection.

"Okay, let's hit the shoe department."

Mildred didn't own one pair of sandals, and it showed. Her feet were pretty, but her toenails left something to be desired.

"Make an appointment for a pedicure," Geneva commented as she peered down at Mildred's bare toenails.

"Okay," Mildred said, and shamefully curled her toes under.

She ended up buying two pairs of wedges with peeka-boo openings.

"Now what?" Geneva said, looking down at her watch. "Lingerie?"

Mildred blushed. She wouldn't dare buy her intimates with Geneva, who represented a motherly figure to her. She just couldn't.

"No, let's go to the watch department."

"Oh, do you need a watch?" Geneva asked as she stopped to admire a pair of stilettos.

"No, I want to buy one for Tony," Mildred said, and started toward the escalator.

Geneva made a face. That statement did not sit well with her. She caught Mildred by the elbow just as she stepped onto the escalator. "Whaddya mean, you want to buy *him* a watch?"

"Just a little gift," Mildred responded without looking at her.

A little gift? A little keepsake to say, Thanks for fucking me? Thanks for paying me some mind?

Geneva bit down on her tongue. She wouldn't say a word. Mildred was a grown-ass woman. She made her own money and had every right to spend it in any way she chose.

Mildred turned and saw the disapproving look on Geneva's face. "What?"

"Nothing, nothing," Geneva said, waving her hand at Mildred.

✦

By the time the saleswoman pulled watch number three out of the glass-enclosed case, Geneva had decided she'd seen enough. With each watch Mildred pointed to, the price tag increased.

Geneva couldn't take it anymore. She was about to bust.

"Okay, baby, I've got to get back uptown," she said suddenly as she wrapped her arms around Mildred's shoulders and gave her a tight hug. "I'll see you Monday, okay?"

Mildred hugged her back. "Are you okay?"

Geneva nodded, forced a smile, and gave her a little two-finger wave before strutting off. As she went, two men shot Geneva approving looks.

Mildred sighed; she wanted men to look at her that way. Not even Tony looked at her that way, and he loved her.

"What do you think about this one?" the saleswoman asked in a bored tone as she presented Mildred with a Coach Legacy sports watch.

Mildred eyed the watch; it was very nice. The price tag read $998.00.

She didn't own one thing that cost as much as that watch did.

The saleswoman exhaled deeply and rolled her brown eyes.

"Yes, I'll take it," Mildred said, digging into her purse and pulling out the American Express gold card she'd never used in the five years she'd had it. "He's worth every dime."

◆

"Wow," Tony said, and then hoisted himself up onto his elbow. "It's great."

Great wasn't the word she was hoping for.

They'd just finished making love at her apartment. Tony's skin glistened with perspiration. His penis lay limp on his thigh.

"Do you really like it?" Mildred asked, wrapping the sheet around her body and pulling her knees up to her chest.

"I-I love it, babe," Tony said, and threw a kiss at her before setting the watch down on the nightstand and picking up the remote. He fluffed his pillow and arranged it carefully behind his head before swiftly scrolling through the channels until he found a news program that satisfied him.

She didn't want to complain, but geez, didn't he even want to try it on?

"Aren't you going to try it on?"

"Huh?" Tony said as he turned to her. "What did you say?"

"Nothing," Mildred said sweetly, and focused her eyes on the newscaster. She could see Tony still watching her.

"Don't be like that, baby," he said. "I didn't hear you."

Mildred swallowed. She was being childish. Men didn't like childish. She would drive him away if she continued to behave that way.

"I-I just said I love you."

Tony grinned. "I love you more, babe."

CHAPTER

Twenty-nine

Tony looked at the caller ID of his phone. Mildred's number glowed on the dark face for the third time. He knew if he didn't answer, she would keep calling. He could turn the phone off, but that would be suspicious to Mildred, and Zebby had warned him that he had her in the place they needed to have her and that he'd better not do anything to fuck it up.

He turned and looked at Liz Choi, the woman he'd met on the street with Errol some weeks earlier. They'd played phone tag for weeks before finally hooking up. And now she lay there beside him in all her naked glory.

"I got to answer this," Tony said, giving her an apologetic look.

Liz raised her hand and nodded toward the diamond-encrusted wedding band she wore. "You know I understand," she said. "Just keep it short."

Tony grinned at her and flipped the phone open.

"Hey, baby, what's up?" he asked in a groggy voice as he padded out of the bedroom and into the living room.

"Did I wake you?" Mildred asked timidly.

"Yeah, yeah, but that's okay. Something wrong?"

There wasn't anything wrong. Mildred just needed to hear his voice.

"No, I just . . . I just . . ." She couldn't finish, she felt so stupid. It was nearly midnight but she hadn't been able to sleep, her mind was racing with thoughts of Tony.

"You miss me?" Tony said as he sat down on the couch and rubbed his head. This was getting old, and fast. He was tired of the constant calls at work, the late-night calls, the text messages, the dinners, and he was so over the sex!

He was sick and tired of all of it.

Mildred's heart skipped a beat. "Yes, I do. Can you come over?"

Tony rolled his eyes. "Now?"

"Yes."

Liz walked in and stood in front of him, her twat inches from his face. He shook his head and gently pushed her away.

"Nah, it's too late and you know we both have to get up early in the morning."

Mildred was hurt.

Liz stepped forward again, this time pushing her bush into his face, muffling his next set of words.

"What, Tony? What? I can't hear you." Mildred's voice was panicked.

Tony covered the phone with his hand, "Look, just give me a minute, okay?"

Liz folded her hands high on her chest and pouted.

"Nothing, baby. I didn't say anything."

"It's just that I miss you so much. I wish you were here with me. I wish we could make love right now," Mildred whined into the phone just as Liz dropped down onto her knees and took Tony's dick into her mouth.

Tony swallowed a moan.

"You—you do?" he croaked.

Mildred pressed the phone against her ear. "Tony? What's going on? What's happening over there?"

"I-I'm touching myself and thinking of you."

Boy, could he think fast on his feet.

"Phone sex?" Mildred said.

Well, she was a pro at phone sex!

She hurriedly ran over to the dresser and pulled out her vibrator. Jumping back into bed, she wiggled out of her underwear and fluffed her pillows to position herself.

"Are you still there, Mildred?" Tony's voice was guttural.

"I'm still here, baby," Mildred responded as she flipped the switch on and began rolling the tip of the vibrator over her clitoris.

Tony had one hand on the back of Liz's head while the other clutched the phone. The pleasure he was deriving from the blow job combined with Mildred's ecstasy-filled cries was taking him to a place he'd never been before.

Just as he felt himself about to explode, Liz removed her mouth. Tony's head jerked up and he mouthed, "What are you doing?"

Liz gave him a mischievous grin and walked away. Tony let out a heavy sigh.

"Baby?" Mildred called to him from the other end of the line.

"Yes, I'm here," Tony said as he looked down at his quickly deflating penis.

"Does it feel good?" Mildred crooned as she worked the vibrator inside her.

"Yes, yes," Tony said as he wrapped his hands around his penis and began to stroke it.

Liz reappeared, walked over to Tony, and tossed a condom into his lap. Tony quickly retrieved it and used his teeth and spare hand to remove the prophylactic from the package. Liz watched as he slipped it onto his penis.

Then he spread his legs and cautioned her to remain quiet by pressing his index finger to his lips.

Liz climbed on, slipped Tony's penis up into her, and began to ride him so vehemently, Tony couldn't help but cry out in pleasure.

"Yes, baby, yes!" Mildred screamed from her apartment. "I'm coming, I'm coming!" Mildred's body bucked up and down.

Tony just grunted, one arm wrapped tightly around Liz's waist, all of his words backed up in his throat as struggled to keep up with Liz's wild pace.

"*Toooonnnnnny!*" Mildred cried as her body rushed to a shattering climax.

At the sound of Mildred's voice, Tony's body went stiff and then shook uncontrollably.

Mildred was panting on the other end of the line.

"Did you come?" Mildred asked when she'd finally caught her breath.

"Y-yes, I did," Tony muttered as he stared deeply into Liz's eyes.

Liz gave Tony a satisfied smile before climbing off him and disappearing into the bedroom.

Tony watched her walk away, then dropped his head onto the back of the couch. He'd forgotten Mildred was on the phone and had begun to slip into slumber when her words pulled him back.

"Do you love me, Tony? I mean, for real?"

Tony shook his head no, but his mouth uttered, "Yes, of course I do."

"Why? Why do you love me?"

He knew it was coming.

"I love you because you're the only woman I ever felt completely safe with. You're my best friend, Mildred. You're the best thing that has ever happened to me."

Mildred tossed the vibrator aside and sat up.

"Oh, Tony," she breathed, and he sensed more than heard the tears in her voice. It was at that moment that he knew he had her hook, line, and sinker and could in effect ask her for anything and everything and she would not deny him.

"See you tomorrow, then?"

"Yes," Mildred said, and then sniffed. "Good night."

"Good night, Mildred," Tony said, and then for added effect blew a kiss into the phone before gently closing the cover.

"Hey," the beauty yelled at him from the bedroom, "are you coming back to bed or what?"

CHAPTER

Thirty

The sex with Liz had gotten a bit wild, so wild that somehow—Tony didn't know exactly how—his face had ended up running smack into the headboard, and now he had a hell of a shiner.

He'd been pissed in the beginning, but halfway into the city, he suddenly realized how that black eye could help him.

Now, sitting across from Mildred, he explained, "You see, Mildred, I made a really bad investment a few months ago." He paused as the lie grew in his mind. "A bad real estate investment. That's why I had to go upstate a few weeks ago."

Mildred nodded as she stared intently at his bruised eye.

"And in order to buy into the investment I had to borrow the money from some really shady guys, and now I'm overdue, and well, this," he said, pointing to his eye, "is the first reminder of that."

Tony watched as Mildred's face began to pulsate with terror.

He took her hand in his and said, "If I don't get them their money and soon, I'm in serious trouble."

Mildred's eyes nearly popped out of her skull. "Oh my God," she said, clutching her chest with her free hand.

She had money saved. She would lend it to him—hell, she would give it to him.

"How much?"

Tony swallowed hard as he searched for just the right amount. "One hundred and fifty Gs."

Mildred didn't have quite that much. "I have eighty," she said.

Tony's eyebrow raised. "Eighty what?"

"Eighty thousand," she said.

"Shit."

Who knew?

"I-I can't take your money, Mildred. I just don't know what I'm going to do," he said with a mournful look on his face.

"Yes, of course you can. Of course you can take my money," Mildred wailed. "I love you and you love me— this is what people who love each other do for one another."

He turned his head dramatically away. "I can't."

Mildred flew from her seat and ran to his side. Bending

over, she pressed her cheek against his and whispered, "You can and you will."

Tony almost laughed—he felt like he'd stepped into a Harlequin romance novel. The drama was just too much.

"What can I do?" Mildred's eyes were glistening with tears now. "Tell me how I can help you. I'll do anything."

✦

Zebby was grinning and rubbing his chin the entire time Tony relayed the story, like some wise old teacher pleased with his student.

When Tony was done, Zebby applauded him.

"Very good, very good," he said.

That evening Zebby and Tony met up at the Blue Water Grill for a meal of sushi and Sauvignon Blanc.

Zebby dabbed the corners of his mouth with his handkerchief.

"So she's totally cool with risking her job and her freedom for you?"

Tony nodded his head proudly.

"Drop your pants, man," Zebby demanded, his voice stern.

"What?"

"I said get up and drop your goddamn pants," Zebby barked. A few of the other diners turned and shot them a quizzical look.

Tony just stared. He didn't quite know what was going on. Then a twinkle appeared in Zebby's eyes and he began to roar with laughter.

"Tone, I figure you must have a diamond-tipped dick to make that bitch risk life and limb for you, and, shit. I ain't seen that before. Me myself, I was only blessed with a gold tip."

Tony began to laugh, and they gave each other some dap across the table.

"You're a sick motherfucker, you know that?" Tony said before reaching for his chopsticks.

Thirty-one

A week passed and Tony was beginning to have second thoughts again. He was having bad dreams about being jailed with a bald, brawly man named Butch who was demanding to see his diamond-tipped penis.

Zebby had tried his best to assure him, taking him step by step through the process. Tony would pick an account and as usual research the beneficiaries on it. After finding none, he would then enter one of the names and social security numbers Zebby had given him, along with a fake death certificate of the person who had originally opened the account.

Mildred would then intercept the paperwork that he'd initialed, forging Mr. Henderson's signature and forwarding it on to the Clearing department, where the request would be double-checked. And then, if everything was hunky-dory (and there was no reason that it shouldn't be), the money would be released to the bank account provided.

Easy as pie.

They'd targeted thirty different accounts, none of which held more than sixty or seventy thousand dollars. Pennies to a big firm like Greene Investments. Each of the targeted accounts had been dormant for more than five years.

Tony wanted to know why they couldn't just hit one of the larger accounts. "Why not get a million dollars in one fell swoop?" he'd asked.

Zebby advised that hitting one of the larger accounts would set off too many bells.

"You've been turning over what, three accounts a week?"

Tony had nodded.

"So you'll continue at that speed. This way no one will be the wiser."

"Okay, but where will the money go? All into the same account?"

"No, that would invite investigation. I've set up thirty different accounts around the country, small banks," Zebby said.

So it was all set up.

Tony put through two small requests and then waited like a virgin on her wedding night. He expected the feds to bust through the doors, handcuff him, and take him away.

But three days later, Zebby called and said, "Montana and South Dakota just hit."

One Month Later...

✦

Thirty-two

Mildred was just staring at him.

"Well, say something."

Mildred took a deep breath and then said, "You lied to me?"

Tony shook his head. "Say something else. You've already said that twice."

They were in her apartment, Tony seated on the couch, Mildred hovering over him, her hands resting on her wide hips as she glared down at him.

"You told me you were in debt for a hundred thousand dollars. I pass on paperwork allowing a hundred thousand dollars to disappear from clients' accounts, and when I say, 'Fine, we're done, you're safe,' you tell me different. You tell me it's actually two hundred thousand?"

Tony's mouth dropped open, but nothing came out.

"Maybe that's a lie too!" Mildred shrieked.

Mildred never yelled, and the sound of her own voice reaching such a shrill crescendo made her jump.

"Baby," Tony started, catching Mildred by her forearms and pulling her stomach into his face, "I'm sorry I lied to you, but I was so ashamed, so very ashamed," he mumbled into the fabric of her dress.

Mildred melted. She sighed and placed her hands on his head, stroking the fine short hairs there.

"You don't ever have to lie to me, Tony. Never." She sighed.

When Tony looked up at her his eyes were brimming with tears.

That got her every time.

"Oh, baby," she said, and her own eyes began to tear. "It's going to be okay." She dropped down to her knees and embraced him.

✦

"So what's going to happen when we get to the two-hundred-thousand-dollar mark?" Zebby asked.

Tony hadn't thought that far ahead. "I don't know, man, I don't know," he said into his cell phone as he navigated his way down Wall Street toward work.

And he didn't know.

What he did know was that the entire situation was wearing on him. The job, the scam, Mildred.

But every time he'd decided he'd had enough and was

going to call Zebby and tell him just that, Zebby would always inform him that another deposit had hit.

It had been a month and Tony hadn't seen a dime and so was beginning to think that Zebby was playing him for a fool, the same way he was playing Mildred.

"Yo, Zebby, funds are little low, if you know what I mean?"

Tony didn't want to come right out and ask for his share—it seemed punkish—but shit, he was the one who was putting his ass on the line every single day he walked into Greene Investments.

He was under a lot of stress and had noticed he wasn't just losing sleep but was losing weight.

"I got your stuff right here. That was my reason for calling, but you started on Mildred before I could even tell you."

Now he really did feel like a punk.

"I'll be there tonight," he said just as he pushed through the wide glass doors of the building and found Mildred standing there, waiting for him as usual.

Tony flipped the phone closed, smiled at Mildred, and started to make small talk as fellow employees milled around waiting for the elevator.

He pretended to listen as Mildred droned on and on about some damn television show she'd watched last night.

His mind was on what Zebby had said about the money.

He'd arranged it so that they would get paid in gold bullion. He didn't know why they couldn't have cash, but

Zebby said the man he'd got to wash the money for him had said this was better, not as easily traced as cash.

Tony had never in his life seen gold bullion, much less held one. The thought of it made his dick go stiff.

Mildred saw the bulge in his pants and blushed. Who had known she'd one day have that kind of effect on a man!

CHAPTER

Thirty-three

Mildred was beaming.

She couldn't stop staring at the ring. Even though it was one of the smallest diamonds she'd ever seen, and the band was thin and cheap-looking, it was an engagement ring.

She held her hand out in front of her face and wiggled her fingers. She was a fiancée!

"Oh, Tony," she gushed, "I can't believe it. I just can't believe it!" She squealed and threw her arms around him, crushing him in a bear hug.

She was ecstatic, even though she'd wished he'd taken her someplace romantic, someplace where people could see her being proposed to. She wanted the entire fairy tale, but she supposed the living room of her apartment would have to do.

"So, shall we plan a date?" she said, still staring lovingly down at the diamond chip.

Tony groaned inwardly. It was never enough, was it?

"Sure, babe—you just tell me where and when and I'll be there."

CHAPTER

Thirty-four

"Get out!" Seneca roared, shoving Mildred halfway across the room.

"Ouch," Mildred screeched as she fell down onto the sofa.

Seneca's eyes were as wide as saucers and her mouth hung open so that Mildred could see her pink tongue.

"Let me see it again," Seneca said, starting toward Mildred.

Mildred stretched her hand out for Seneca to see.

"Humph. He could have spent a little more, don't you think?" Seneca remarked sarcastically.

Mildred pulled her hand away.

"Fuck you, you hater," Mildred spat.

Seneca drew back in shock. She couldn't remember ever hearing Mildred curse. "You're certainly picking up some nasty habits, Mildred Johnson."

"Sorry," Mildred said, and then huffed, "but you deserved that. You never seem to be happy for me. Here I've found this wonderful man and he loves me for me and wants to marry me, and all you can say is that he could have spent a little more money? Love is not about money, Seneca. It's about what you have in here," Mildred said, slapping her chest.

Seneca smirked. "Yeah, okay. Congratulations," she said halfheartedly.

"Well, you know, if you can't be happy for me, I don't think we can continue to be friends," Mildred said.

For the second time that evening Seneca drew back in shock.

Yeah, she was gagging on the inside. Envious. She couldn't understand how it was that overweight, uglyducking Mildred had snagged a man as fine as Tony.

"I said congratulations," Seneca snapped, snatching her handbag from the coffee table. "I don't know what you want from me. Maybe you want me to kiss your ass, huh?"

Mildred said nothing.

"Well, I'm not going to do it. And if me not kissing your ass means we can't be friends anymore, then so be it," Seneca said as she turned and marched toward the front door. "Have a nice fucking life," she threw over her shoulder as she stormed out into the hallway and down the stairs.

Mildred didn't feel a drop of regret. She calmly walked over to the door and secured the lock. She didn't need Seneca or anyone else for that matter. All she needed was Tony.

A Series of Fortunate Events . . .

✦

CHAPTER

Thirty-five

She knew she was going against everything he'd asked her not to do, but it was her wedding day and she wanted it to be special.

Mildred had wanted a big to-do. A church wedding and reception at the Grand Prospect Hall.

She'd gone for a showing and even a food tasting, claiming that Tony, her husband-to-be, was an investment banker who traveled a lot, which is why she was there alone.

But Tony said a large wedding would call attention to them and they were almost home free with an extra hundred grand to start a new life with.

So a civil service wedding, Tony said, would be the best thing.

Quick and quiet.

And then off on their two-week honeymoon to Bora Bora.

✦

"You're getting what?" Geneva choked out after having taken a sip of her Diet Pepsi.

They were eating lunch at McDonald's.

"Married!" Mildred squealed, thrusting the ring in Geneva's face.

Geneva squinted at the tiny diamond.

"To that man? That Tony guy?"

Mildred rapidly bobbed her head up and down as she bit down into a Big Mac.

Geneva didn't know what to say. She was mute with shock. But after some time, she finally said, "Well, congratulations. When's the big day?"

"Tomorrow at noon."

Geneva blinked. "Tomorrow? So soon. And where?"

"City Hall."

Geneva had always been suspicious of this relationship, but now the hairs were standing up on the back of her neck.

She leaned forward, locked her eyes with Mildred's, and asked, "Is he a citizen?"

Mildred's head jerked with surprise. "Of course he is!"

"Then why all the rush? Why can't you two wait and have a proper ceremony?"

Mildred's response was sharp: "Because we don't want to wait."

Geneva shrank back into her seat. What ever happened to the sweet, timid Mildred she once knew?

"Makes sense," Geneva squeaked as she reached for a french fry.

"And I hope you'll be able to attend?"

"Wouldn't miss it for the world."

CHAPTER

Thirty-six

That Friday was gray and muggy with a threatening sky.

The plan was to get married at noon and then go out and have a wonderful lunch before Tony headed back to the office to finish up some work.

Mildred, on the other hand, had the day off, and she would head back home and prepare the apartment for a wonderful romantic evening.

They would fly out first thing Saturday morning to spend ten blissful days in Bora Bora. After that they would return to work for at least another three months before handing in their resignations and disappearing completely.

Mildred had made up beautiful wedding invitations on

the computer and handed one to Geneva as well as to her boss, Mr. Henderson.

Mildred arrived in full wedding dress, via gypsy cab.

When she waltzed into the main hall of the courthouse, heads turned and people snickered, but all Mildred heard were the harps inside her head.

"Y-you look lovely," Geneva heard herself lie. Mildred looked like a float from the Thanksgiving Day Parade.

"Who did your makeup?"

Geneva had to ask because Mildred had on the thickest press-on eyelashes she'd ever seen. And to add insult to injury, she'd applied a heavy dose of rose-colored blush to her cheeks. She looked like a clown.

Her lipstick was the best thing going—a soft, glittery pink.

"I did," Mildred announced proudly as she embraced Geneva.

Clutching her six-foot-long train, she wobbled over to Mr. Henderson, who was so rigid with shock, he could barely raise his arms.

"You look . . . um . . . glorious," Mr. Henderson said.

"Thank you!"

Couple after happy couple walked into the matrimony room and walked out husband and wife. It was a quarter past twelve and Tony still hadn't arrived.

"It shouldn't be much longer," Mildred stalled. "I think he said he was driving in today."

Geneva and Mr. Henderson nodded.

By twelve-thirty, Mildred had dialed Tony's cell phone

three times, but each time it had gone straight to voice mail.

Her spirits still high, she made more excuses.

By quarter of one Mr. Henderson announced that he had an important meeting to attend at one o'clock and couldn't wait anymore.

"Mildred, dear, I'm so sorry, but I have to go," he said, checking his watch. "I wish I could be here to witness this wonderful occasion, but . . ."

Mildred waved him off. "Oh, Mr. Henderson, don't be sorry. It means so much to me that you waited this long. But I'm sure he'll be here soon."

Mildred was still smiling.

"I'm sure," Mr. Henderson said as he handed her an envelope and then patted her hand.

He shot Geneva an unsure look before he walked away.

Geneva looked at her watch. It was one o'clock and Mildred was beginning to look worried. Geneva herself had had a sinking feeling as soon as she walked into the building. Now it was more than obvious to her that Tony was standing Mildred up.

Mildred jabbed the redial button on her phone, listened as it went to voice mail, pressed End Call, and then jabbed the redial button again.

This psychotic repetitive behavior went on for fifteen minutes straight before Geneva built up the courage to approach her friend.

"Mildred—" she started, resting a comforting hand on Mildred's shoulder.

Mildred shrugged her hand off. "He's just late, stuck

somewhere, that's all," she mumbled, and then turned on Geneva and screamed, "He'll be here!"

Geneva jumped back. Mildred was having a nervous breakdown right before her eyes.

At two o'clock, Mildred came completely undone, sliding down the marble wall and settling into a weeping mess on the floor.

Geneva went to her, stooped down beside her, took her hand in hers, and said, "C'mon, girl. Let's go."

Mildred snatched her hand back. "You go on, Geneva. He'll be here, I know he will."

Geneva felt horrible leaving her there, but she had a job that she liked and needed, and she'd already been gone for two hours.

"I'll call you later," Geneva said, after giving Mildred a hug and stepping into the waiting elevator.

By four o'clock the sky had opened up, soaking Mildred to the bone as she walked slowly toward the subway.

CHAPTER

Thirty-seven

So what are you going to do with your money, man?"
They'd actually walked away with a million and a
half dollars. Tony had only exchanged a hundred thousand dollars' worth of his gold bullion; the rest he'd
socked away in a safe-deposit box.

"Me," Tony said with a smile, "I'm going to ride off
into the sunset."

The sunset for Tony was Barbados. His birthplace. His
mother had a vacant lot on the popular western coast of
the island, directly across from the ocean, and he was going to build his dream house on it.

He'd told his mother that Greene Investments was
opening an office on the island and that he had been chosen to run it.

Barbados was booming, and the cost of living had sky-rocketed, but his American dollar was worth double there, and he had plans to start a business. He was going to buy a few Jet Skis and then a small yacht and while away his days drinking rum punch and romancing beautiful women, until he found the right one.

The right one.

The one he would marry and start a family with. That's what he was going to do.

"What about you, Zebby? What are you going to do?"

Zebby laughed. "If I tell you, I'm going to have to kill you."

He seemed to be joking, but something in Tony told him that Zebby wasn't being completely humorous.

"So when do you ride off into the sunset?" Zebby asked as he refilled Tony's snifter with cognac.

"Tomorrow morning at seven A.M."

Thirty-eight

Three days had passed by the time Geneva had the superintendent of the building open Mildred's door and they walked in to find her, still dressed in her wedding gown, sprawled out on the living room floor.

The superintendent's eyes bulged. "Is she dead?"

Geneva rushed to her side and fell down to her knees, screaming, "Oh Lord, don't let her be dead!" as she started violently shaking her.

"What?" Mildred muttered, her blood-shot eyes slowly opening.

Geneva let go a sigh of relief. "Oh, thank goodness."

And then Geneva made a face. "Your breath smells like shit," she said, waving her hands in front of her nose. "Have you been drinking?"

"Yes. Look," the superintendent announced, using one of the thousand keys on the ring he held to point at the evidence.

Lined up neatly along the side of the couch were five empty bottles of champagne.

Geneva struggled to her feet. "Thank you, Mr. Rodriguez. You can go now," she said as she ushered him toward the door.

"You sure? Maybe she needs her stomach pumped."

"No, no, I'm sure she's fine."

"Maybe"—Mr. Rodriguez turned to face Geneva—"she *loco* in her *cabeza?*" he said, pointing to his head.

When she'd finally gotten Mr. Rodriguez out of the apartment, Geneva went back to Mildred.

"Get up," she said, grabbing Mildred by the hand and tugging. "Get up and pull yourself together."

Mildred looked a mess. Her hair lay helter-skelter all over her head and her lips were puffed and swollen.

Reluctantly, Mildred struggled to her feet. Filthy streaks and something that looked like blood splotches were all over the wedding gown and the bodice looked like it had been torn.

"What happened to you?" Geneva asked, pointing to the damage on the dress and then her wreck of a mouth.

Mildred looked down at it as if surprised before the memory floated back to her. "I couldn't get it off and so I tried to cut my way out of it," she slurred as Geneva guided her toward the bathroom.

When they got to the bathroom, Geneva noticed that it wasn't just the alcohol that was making Mildred slur.

"What happened to your teeth!"

Mildred's two front teeth were missing, leaving a gaping dark space.

Mildred touched her mouth. "Oh," she moaned, "I tripped coming up from the train station and fell right on my face."

Well, Geneva guiltily thought as she helped Mildred out of the wedding gown, that certainly isn't the worst thing that could have happened to her.

An hour later, Mildred sat on the couch, wrapped in her terry cloth robe, sipping tea. The sobbing would stop and start and then stop again. Geneva held her hand the entire time, forbidding herself to say "I told you so."

"He's a piece of shit," Geneva spat. "A low-down dirty dog."

Mildred flinched with every word.

"This too shall pass," Geneva said, her voice taking on a softer tone. "It'll be tough, but you're strong and you'll survive this," she said, patting her hand. "And don't you worry, Mildred—he'll get his. Karma is a bitch."

✦

She couldn't go back to work. Couldn't face her coworkers and certainly not her boss. So she swore Geneva to secrecy. Told her to tell people that she'd spoken to her and that she and Tony were off on their honeymoon. She needed time to collect herself, to think about how she was going to right this terrible wrong.

A million and a half dollars. A million and a half dollars.

The numbers danced in her head day and night, threatening to drive her insane.

Why hadn't she stopped at one hundred thousand?

Why had she agreed to do this at all?

Love was a strange thing. Love made you do shit you wouldn't normally do. And she had loved him, had loved him more than she loved herself, and he had fucked her over—used her and thrown her away like a piece of stale bread.

And he'd made her look like a fool. Like a goddamn fool—and not only that. He'd turned her into a criminal!

He would pay. She didn't know how, but he would.

Mildred kept replaying what Geneva had said about karma. But sometimes, Mildred thought to herself, karma took too long to step in.

Sometimes karma didn't jump into action until the next life, and Mildred needed retribution yesterday.

"Oh, you're going to suffer, Anthony Landry!" she screamed out, and shook her fists in the air. "You're going to suffer in the worst way!"

CHAPTER

Thirty-nine

"Well, this certainly is a surprise," Mr. Henderson began as he folded his hands on his desk. "An unpleasant surprise."

"Yes, sir, I'm sorry."

Mildred's eyes swept the floor.

"My . . . um . . . husband wants me to stay at home, and we, well, we want to start a family immediately."

She'd become such a good liar. Such a wonderful actress!

"I see," Mr. Henderson said thoughtfully. "Of course, I hate to see you go. But I do appreciate the thirty-day notice—"

"And"—Mildred took a step forward and interrupted

him—"I will make sure that my replacement is properly trained."

"Well, thank you," Mr. Henderson said.

"It's my pleasure."

Mr. Henderson looked closely at Mildred. There was something different about her.

"You, um . . ." Mr. Henderson wanted to be careful not to offend her, so he fluttered his fingers in front of his mouth. "Something different?"

Mildred smiled broadly, exposing her new set of tooth implants. That's how she'd spent her two-week vacation, not beneath the blue skies of Bora Bora, but in a dentist's office.

Mr. Henderson squinted. The straight teeth made a world of difference in her appearance. She really wasn't so hard to look at now. Now only if she lost some weight . . .

"Very nice, Mildred. Very nice."

"Thank you, Mr. Henderson."

✦

Mildred would use the next few weeks to bury, as much as possible, any paperwork that would link her to the crime. During that time she found out that Tony had handed in his resignation two weeks before they were to be married.

"He never had any intention of marrying me!" she wailed over the phone to Geneva. "He just wanted the money—"

Mildred caught herself, but not in time for Geneva to have missed the implication.

"What money?" Geneva asked.

She couldn't tell Geneva the truth. If she did and the crime was discovered, the FBI would question everyone who worked at the firm, and Geneva might crack under the questioning and then she could be considered a co-conspirator.

"I-I gave him some money out of my pension fund." Mildred felt her recovery was brilliant.

"Oh, Mildred," Geneva groaned. "How could you?"

"I know, I know. It was a stupid thing to do."

"How much did you give him?"

Mildred bit down hard on her bottom lip and then whispered, "Ten thousand dollars."

Geneva went silent.

"Geneva? Geneva?"

"I'm still here," Geneva breathed. "Well, that's a lot of money, but money can always be replaced. He could have taken something more precious."

"Like what?"

Geneva sighed. "Your spirit, sweetie. Your spirit is the most precious thing you own, and he could have taken that away from you."

It was Mildred's turn to be quiet.

"You've got to start putting yourself first, Mildred. Take this experience as a lesson. Use this lesson to move your life forward, to begin again."

Mildred nodded and said she would do just that.

✦

The weeks inched by and Mildred didn't know what it
was she was going to do with herself once she left Greene
Investments. As she and Geneva strolled down Broadway,
Geneva suggested that she move away.

"Like to Queens?" Mildred said.

"No, like to another city. How about Atlanta or Los
Angeles?"

Mildred didn't know about any of that. But she did
agree that she needed a change.

"Maybe a vacation?" Geneva suggested.

A vacation. Traveling the world had been a lifelong
dream of hers. Maybe that's what she would do.

"I have a friend," Geneva started as she dug into her
purse and pulled out her cell phone, "who's the assistant
manager at this boutique hotel in Barbados. It's the slow
season now, and I'm sure she'll be able to give you a good
deal on a room."

"Really?" Mildred said hopefully.

"Yeah. I think a little sunshine and seawater is all you
need to help get you off to a new start."

Geneva dialed the number, waited a minute, and then
said, "Hey, Chevy, this is Geneva. I need a favor . . ."

Part Two

◆

Part Two

CHAPTER

Forty

Tony stood at the water's edge, a Banks beer in one hand, while the other shielded his eyes against the bright rays of the setting sun.

There were still a few tourists on the beach, slowly gathering their belongings as they prepared to make their way back to their rented beach homes and hotel rooms to prepare for dinner.

He waved to them as they moved past him. Most he knew by name. Some of the newer faces he would know by the week's end.

Tony was the man they all had to come to sooner or later.

He owned three of the fastest personal watercrafts on the island: Matlock 6000s—illegal to operate on the island of Barbados, but he'd paid off the right people and so it had cleared customs quicker than a soda through a straw.

A week into his operation and he was being harassed by a few of the guys who were angry due to all of the business Tony had stolen away from them. Again, Tony greased a few official palms, some threats were made, a few heads were cracked, and that was the end of that.

Now Tony was king of the beach. Or at least that's the way he felt.

"Is that it?" A tall, coal-colored fellow with blond locks and gold teeth strolled up beside him.

"Yeah, that's it for the day."

The man was born Miguel Braithwait but went by the nickname Bon Jovi—Bon for short.

It seemed to Tony that everyone on the island had a nickname; no one seemed to be known by a birth name.

Bon owned a Toyota 4×4, which he used to tow boats and Jet Skis. He also had a large backyard where he stored cars and Jet Skis, all for a fee.

Bon stared out at the now dark blue horizon. "Good day?"

"It's always a good day in Bimsha." Tony laughed and slapped Bon hard on his bare back.

Bimsha, Little England . . . Barbados itself had a number of nicknames. He loved being back home, loved the bright sun-filled days and the long, dark, warm nights. It was a sexual place filled with brazen, beautiful wide-hipped women, and men gathered outside the rum shops arguing about who had the biggest dick and how many virgins they'd slain in their lifetime.

Tony had been on the island for two months. The house he had started to build wouldn't be ready for another six to nine months, so he was renting a small two-bedroom, two-bath bungalow in Paynes Bay, across the street from the beach.

Life was good. Shit, life was great!

He had fresh food, clean air, and more women than he knew what to do with.

Now as he stood on the beach, the warm water lapping at his toes as the first few stars made their appearance in the dark sky, he felt untouchable. Invincible. He felt like God himself.

CHAPTER

Forty-one

Dressed in a blue and yellow tracksuit, dark glasses, and wide-brimmed straw hat, Mildred clomped toward the gate in her white espadrilles, her massive thighs rubbing loudly together as she went.

She'd arrived at the airport three hours early and now settled herself down in a chair situated right in front of the door that would lead her and the other passengers onto the plane.

She'd stopped in the magazine shop and bought loads of reading material, but now as she flipped anxiously through the magazines, she found she couldn't concentrate on anything but the adventure ahead of her.

Twenty minutes to boarding, Mildred had to pee, but

she was afraid to move. Afraid she might miss the boarding call for her flight.

She sat perfectly still, her passport and ticket clutched tightly in her right hand, willing the pressing need to urinate to disappear.

But the more she wished it away, the more urgent it became.

Finally, unable to bear it any longer, she jumped from her seat and bolted down the corridor, searching frantically for the bathroom.

Upon her return, she found to her dismay that her seat had been taken. The young, blond-haired boy looked up from his video game and stuck his tongue out at her.

"Flight seventeen eighty-five to Barbados is ready for boarding."

Mildred stared down at her ticket. Her heart began to flutter.

"American would like to welcome their first-class passengers and elite card holder members to board at this time."

Mildred was a first-class passenger. She figured her first trip abroad should be special and so had forked over the extra grand it cost to go top of the line.

The little blond boy was screaming, "Let's go, let's go!" as his mother tried in vain to calm him down.

"Not yet, honey. We're not in first class," the woman said as her face turned three shades of red.

As Mildred moved past them, she caught the eye of the little boy, who was glowering at her. Mildred discreetly gave him the finger.

"Good morning," the gate agent greeted her as she took Mildred's ticket and slipped it through the machine. "Have a wonderful flight."

Mildred's ticket stated that she was in seat 2B.

A window seat.

She slipped in. The seat was too small: the armrests cut dangerously into her fleshy waist and to make it worse the seat belt refused to clasp over her large stomach.

Mildred tugged and tugged. She tugged so hard, her hand slipped from the strap and banged into the wall.

The boarding passengers giggled behind their hands as an embarrassed Mildred shrank into her seat.

A smiling red-headed flight attendant approached and immediately saw what the problem was. She raised her finger, winked, and walked away.

When she returned, she was holding another belt in her hand.

"This is an extender belt," she said as she leaned over Mildred and fumbled around her waist for a moment before standing up and exclaiming, "Voilà!"

Mildred looked down; she was now strapped safely in.

"It's a miracle," she heard herself say.

✦

Twenty minutes later, flight 1785 climbed into the blue yonder.

Mildred swallowed her screams, squeezed her eyes shut, and clutched the armrests with all of her might.

When the plane leveled and the Fasten Seat Belt light went off, the flight attendant, whose name Mildred had learned was Julie, came around and offered her a beverage of her choice.

"Champagne?"

After three glasses of champagne, a hot towel, a bowl of exotic nuts, and a steak dinner followed by a bowl of vanilla ice cream topped with chocolate fudge, Mildred began to feel her nervousness slip away.

She donned the headset and settled back to watch the in-flight movie. Before she realized it, Julie was gently shaking her shoulder, advising her that they were about to land and would she please bring her seat back into the upright and locked position.

Mildred raised the shade and looked down. The island loomed below them and she could see the plane's shadow hovering over the lush greenery.

Her heart caught in her throat. The water was the exact same color as it was in her beloved travel magazines!

The heat gripped her as soon as she stepped down onto the tarmac. Holding tight to her hat, she fell in line with the other passengers as they began their ten-minute-long hike to the receiving hall.

"First time here?" The immigration officer eyed her.

Mildred nodded nervously. Maybe he knew what she'd done back in New York. Maybe she was a wanted woman and didn't even know it.

The immigration officer bowed his head and scrutinized her paperwork and passport.

"Where are you staying?"

Mildred's mind instantly went blank. It was a strange name.

"I, uh . . ." Mildred stalled as she dug into her massive canvas bag in search of the hotel voucher.

"Never mind, never mind," the officer said impatiently as he handed Mildred her passport and waved her away.

Mildred hoped they all weren't as rude as the immigration officer.

Taking her place alongside the carousel, Mildred thought that maybe the champagne and the excitement of traveling for the first time was taking a toll on her imagination, because the redcaps were walking slowly behind, pushing their dollies and staring at her ass!

"Nice," one murmured.

"Dat ding there look good for ridin'," another said.

Mildred casually looked over her shoulder and checked out her behind. One of the redcaps saw her looking and said, "Yeah, it's nice, all right."

Mildred smiled in spite of herself.

CHAPTER

Forty-two

Mildred stood beneath the shaded area alongside the taxi stand, people-watching. She was still very nervous, but she was also thrilled and giddy with excitement.

A tall, slim, bronze-complexioned woman with long, straight black hair approached.

"Mildred?"

Mildred nodded her head.

The woman leaned dramatically back on one leg and spouted, "You're a big old girl, huh?"

Those few words sent Mildred plummeting back to earth. She turned and looked back at the door she'd just exited from. Mildred wanted to be back in there among the luggage carousels and the flattering remarks about her ass.

" 'Scuse me?"

"Geneva said you were a big girl . . . but damn . . ." the woman exclaimed as she started a slow stroll around Mildred.

"Oh, you must be Chevy?" Mildred said when they were face-to-face again.

Geneva had warned her about Chevy's sharp tongue.

"Yes, I am, and you are *definitely* Mildred Johnson," Chevy said. "Follow me, please."

Mildred followed Chevy across the road toward the parking lot. The sun was intense, and Mildred found herself breathing heavily as she struggled to carry her suitcase.

"Nice car," Mildred commented as she climbed into the passenger side of the silver Mercedes-Benz.

"Yes, it is," Chevy sang. "It belongs to my boss."

"Oh," Mildred breathed as she unzipped her jacket.

As Chevy threw the car into drive, she scrutinized Mildred out of the corner of her eye. In her opinion, Mildred looked a hot mess. Who ever heard of pairing a tracksuit with espadrilles?

"You'll feel the air in a minute or two."

Mildred was fanning herself with her hands.

"So, your boss, does he own more than one hotel?"

"Yeah, there's Chimbarosa here in Barbados and Bougainvilla over in Bequia."

"Be-who?"

"Bequia. It's a small island south of here. But anyway, Oswald Heath, my boss, is a doctor. This is just his side gig."

"Doctor of what?"

"He's a plastic surgeon," Chevy said, and then mumbled, "Maybe I can get you a consultation."

"I'm sorry, did you say something?" Mildred said, leaning sideways.

"No, nothing."

✦

Chimbarosa was a former slave plantation located in St. Joseph Parish. The doctor had purchased the four-bedroom stone home and its surrounding ten acres, lush with palm and fruit trees, fifteen years earlier. Then he had added one story to the original structure, increasing it to eight bedrooms. He also added a pool and a small open-air restaurant as well as a spa. It had been voted one the best luxury boutique hotels in the world by *Travel + Leisure* on two separate occasions. From what Chevy told her, the hotel had just undergone a multimillion-dollar renovation and had installed a new health program.

A young man dressed in a starched white uniform greeted them at the top of the driveway. Opening Mildred's door, he did a little bow and said, "Welcome," before gracing Mildred with a wide smile. Mildred couldn't remember ever seeing teeth so bright.

The interior of Chimbarosa looked like something out of the movie *Casablanca*, with its dark wooden plank floors and slow-whirling ceiling fans. The shuttered windows were thrown open, allowing the soft breeze to gently stir the sheer white curtains.

As Chevy and Mildred moved toward the front desk area, Mildred allowed her hands to glide across the curved backs of the plantation chairs.

"Welcome, Miss Johnson," the young woman said as she handed her a large bronze skeleton key. "You're in the Calabash Room."

Mildred followed Chevy up the stone steps and down a narrow hallway. There were just four guest rooms on that floor, hidden behind wooden doors that were painted in cool Caribbean colors. The Calabash Room's door was painted foam green.

When Mildred stepped inside, she was sure she heard the theme to *Gone With the Wind* in her head. "Oh my," she proclaimed.

The room was simple elegance. A large plank bed floated in the middle of the room, suspended from the ceiling by coiled pearl-colored rope. There was a small wrought-iron table painted white and then distressed, complete with a vase of tropical flowers. Pale peach walls, mahogany plank floors, a wooden ceiling fan, and a white wicker dressing table with matching chest of drawers completed the room. The bathroom was small but beautiful with its glass tiled walls and claw-foot tub. A terrace overlooked the hotel grounds, but beyond that, Mildred could see the sparkling blue Caribbean Ocean.

"So do you like it?" Chevy asked.

"It's just beautiful," Mildred croaked. She was feeling very emotional, very overwhelmed.

"Good," Chevy breathed, and looked down at her watch. "Well, you've missed lunch, but we do an afternoon tea service with hors d'oeuvres. Wine, cheese, and crackers. That should hold you over until dinner," Chevy said as her eyes rolled over Mildred's body. "Well, at least I hope it will," she said under her breath.

Mildred flopped down onto the bed. She planned on just lying there for a few moments, just long enough to process everything, but in time her eyes grew heavy and she woke to the sound of Chevy calling her name from the other side of the door.

"Mildred, are you okay in there?"

"Yes, yes, I fell asleep," Mildred said, sitting up and rubbing her eyes. She hadn't realized how tired she was. It was probably the stress and fatigue of the last several weeks coming down on her.

"Dinner starts in an hour. I was hoping we could dine together," Chevy said, and then there was a long pause until she added, "So we can talk?"

Mildred didn't know if she liked the sound of that.

CHAPTER
Forty-three

Up until six months ago, Chevy had been doing hair at her mother's Pittsburgh salon. She'd been rattling on and on to one of her favorite customers about her experience in the travel industry.

She knew that her client Vanessa was married to a doctor, but Chevy had no idea the doctor owned two Caribbean boutique hotels.

Vanessa informed her that their assistant manager had just given notice and they were desperate to replace him and she wondered with all of Chevy's experience, if she might be interested.

Just like that!

No interview, just here's your ticket, here's your salary, and bon voyage!

Chevy didn't have to think twice about it. She'd always wanted to live outside of the United States, and she couldn't think of a better place to start than a vibrant Caribbean island like Barbados.

She'd spent the first three months settling in to her new position and getting to know the island and its people, especially the men.

So far she'd had only one sexual encounter on the island, with an island police officer, Justine Hope, a tall chocolate brother who, many said, had a woman in every parish. Chevy had met him at a cocktail reception hosted at Daphne's Restaurant.

Their eyes had locked across the crowded room, and even now Chevy would always remember that as a Hollywood cliché moment.

They'd spent most of the evening walking circles around each other, but just before the night was about to end, he walked over to her and introduced himself.

"I'm Justine Hope. And you are?"

He had the longest lashes she'd ever seen on a man, and a smile that was sexy and sinister. It's true what they say about women knowing in the first five minutes whether or not they're going to give a man some sex, 'cause she knew immediately that she had to have him.

"Chevy Cambridge," she'd replied.

Chevy couldn't remember what all they talked about. Blame that on the bottle of champagne she'd consumed. But she did remember being in the back of his patrol car, her legs thrown over the front seat, Justine Hope on his

knees, between her legs, eating her out like she had something up in her he needed to survive.

And when he finally slipped himself inside her, Chevy
swore she heard harp music. It was probably the best sex
she'd ever had . . . in the back of a car.

Now, as she sat staring at the prisms the candlelight
made through her water glass, awaiting Mildred's arrival,
she shook off the memory and began to muse on what
Geneva had shared with her about what Mildred had been
through.

Geneva had implored Chevy to help Mildred find her
spine, as well as her self-esteem. And if anybody knew a
thing or two about putting one's life back into perspective,
it was Chevy.

"What are you thinking about?" Mildred was standing
at the table.

Chevy grinned up at her. "Life, Mildred. Life."

✦

Mildred perused the menu. There was no red meat
on it, or fried foods. Everything was either boiled, baked,
or steamed. Brown rice and whole grain bread were the
other offerings.

Mildred was disappointed, but she wouldn't let it spoil
her first night on the island. She could have future meals
someplace else, so in the meantime she ordered the seared
salmon.

When her plate arrived she found that it held the
thinnest slice of salmon she'd ever seen. So thin it was al-

most translucent, allowing a clear view to the bed of mixed greens it rested on.

Looking up at Chevy, Mildred said, "I'm going to need more than this."

Chevy plucked a carrot stick from her salad and responded, "Hunger is a state of mind, my dear."

Was this a joke?

From the expression on Chevy's face, it certainly was not.

Mildred looked around the restaurant; everyone's meal resembled hers—light.

"Okay, so this is your program," Chevy said, sliding a thick dark blue folder across the table.

"Program?"

"Yes, program. You'll be up by six. You'll meet with your instructor in the lobby by six-thirty, after which you will go on an hour-long run. Seven-thirty, breakfast—"

"Wait a minute," Mildred squeaked, pushing her glasses back up her nose. "I'm on vacation. I'm not here for a program."

Chevy continued on as if Mildred hadn't uttered a word.

Later that night as she lay in bed, her stomach grumbling with hunger, she quietly cussed Geneva out, and then after that she began to plot her escape.

CHAPTER

Forty-four

Up and at 'em, Mildred Johnson!"

Mildred almost jumped out of her skin.

In front of her stood a blurred figure. After she reached for her glasses and slipped them on, a tall white woman— or at least Mildred thought it was a woman—came into view.

"You were supposed to meet me in the lobby to begin your training. It is now exactly ten minutes past that time!"

Her eyes moved from the bulldog-faced he-she down to the long bamboo stick it held and then up to the blond hair that had been cut close, military-style.

Mildred jumped. "Wh-who are you?"

"I'm Drill Sergeant Baxter. Miriam Baxter."

Whack!

Miriam brought the stick down hard onto her palm.

Mildred jumped and cast a frightened look at the stick.

"You'll be next if you don't get your rump up and out of the bed!"

Mildred released a nervous laugh. She must be dreaming. That was it. The lack of food, the swinging bed, and the new environment—all of that had brought on this crazy nightmare. If she could just wait for a moment, she would wake up and this, including what had happened before this, would all just fade away with the morning light.

Mildred closed her eyes and waited.

Whack!

The stick sliced into the comforter wrapped around Mildred's body, and her eyes popped wide open again.

She guessed it wasn't a dream.

Miriam Baxter leaned in, her steely blue eyes penetrating Mildred's soupy brown ones. "I don't like to repeat myself, soldier—I mean, Mildred," she said before turning on her Nike running sneakers and marching out of the room.

"Five minutes!" she yelled over her shoulder.

✦

By noon, Mildred was hiding in the garden behind an old spoked wheel, desperately trying to get a signal on her cell phone.

She'd been there for close to an hour before the aroma

of food caught her attention. Her stomach groaned. All she'd had for breakfast was a small bowl of raspberries and a protein shake.

She hadn't signed up for this. She wanted out, and now!

Standing up, she moved as swiftly as possible between the trunks of the palm trees, weaving in and out, making her way to the dining room area, where she then slipped quickly into the kitchen.

The staff looked up and someone said, "You know we're not allowed to give you extra portions, don't you?"

And then someone else added, "And we're armed."

Mildred wiped the sweat from her forehead. "I just want to make a call, that's all."

The staff watched her with wary eyes.

CHAPTER

Forty-five

"Chevy!" Chevy's head jerked at the sound of Geneva's frantic voice.

"Why are you screaming?"

"I just got a phone call from Mildred. She said that you're trying to kill her!"

"And you believe her?" Chevy's tone was calm.

"Yes!"

"Geneva, the woman is grief-stricken, among other things. She's just trying to cope with all that has happened to her—"

"Are you saying she's lying?"

"I'm saying that she believes her imagination to be reality—"

"Stop it right now, Chevanese Cambridge."

"Stop what?"

"Stop your lying."

Chevy laughed. "Okay, okay. So we have her on a little weight management program. So what?"

"So what? She's down there on vacation, for goodness' sake! She thinks that I set this whole thing up."

"Well, you did, didn't you?"

"Chevy, I thought she would be swimming and sunning, not running laps around the property!"

"She will do all that other stuff eventually."

"And she told me that the woman in charge of this program is Miriam Baxter. I hope that is not the same woman—"

Chevy pressed the End button on her phone.

She was not in the mood for any of it. But to tell the truth, the Miriam Baxter on the property was the very same one who'd made Geneva's life a living hell a few years earlier when Geneva was in the throes of her weight-loss saga. Miriam Baxter had been one of the head honcho weight loss counselors at Calorie Counters, and she had tormented Geneva. Her idea of an effective weight loss program was threats, bullying, and terrorization. No wonder Geneva had gained twenty pounds instead of losing the ten she'd signed up for.

In the end, someone called the law on Miriam Baxter and she was sentenced to six months behind bars.

After Miriam was released from prison, her physical fitness license was revoked and she was unable to find work anywhere in the United States. She took off for Panama, where she successfully operated a weight management program at a small spa hotel on the coast.

She was hard on the residents—one could even go so far as to say fanatical—but she got results!

And that's all Chevy was thinking when she hired her.

Geneva would see Mildred's miraculous transformation for herself, and then Chevy wouldn't hesitate to bet her bottom dollar that Geneva's fat ass would be on the first plane to Barbados, with bells on!

Forty-six

Hey, Errol, what's going on, man!" Tony sang joyfully into his cell phone.

"Nothing much. How's the king of Barbados doing?"

"Well, you know, what can I say? I'm doing my thang!"

"I hear that."

"So when are you coming down?"

"I'm thinking maybe around Christmastime, but I'm not sure yet."

"That would be the perfect time. You know the island will be popping for sure then, lots of fetes."

"Lots of what?"

"Fetes, man . . . parties."

"You've really gone full-blown coconut, huh?" Errol teased.

"And you know that. So how's things in the Big Apple?"

"Same old, same old, ya know. The grind and the rhythm."

"Yeah, man, and I got tell you, I don't miss the grind or the rhythm."

"Man, you hit the jackpot. Getting an office job like that on an island."

"So, listen—this call is costing me a fortune, so I gotta hop," Tony said.

"You know you can afford it, you cheap-ass Negro!"

"Yeah, whatever—I'll e-mail you."

"Stay tight," Errol said before he hung up.

Tony stuck his cell phone into the plastic protective case around his neck. He was headed to the Blue Monkey for an afternoon snack and a drink. Business was dead today. It was October—hurricane season—and so the rain had been coming down in short but torrential intervals all day long. At the moment, though, the sun was peeking out from between a mass of rain clouds.

Tomorrow would be a better day. The weatherman had called for clear skies, and for the icing on the cake, a cruise ship would be coming in. For Tony that meant at least a $1,500 day.

"How are you?" the pretty brown-skinned bartender welcomed him. "What can I get for you today?"

Tony grinned. Donnette had legs that went on for

miles, and when they did end they rounded out into an ass that was as firm as a basketball. "You," Tony said, leaning over the bar. "Every day I tell you that you can get me you, and all you do is bring me a bottle of Banks beer and a plate of grilled mahimahi and french fries."

Donnette batted her long black lashes at him. "Well, I bring you that because I know that's all you *really* want," she said with a sly smile as she set the Banks down before Tony.

Tony lifted the bottle and drank deeply as he watched her strut off.

He wanted her; there was no denying that.

She was fine as hell and had a shape to die for, but the downside was that she'd been with most of the men on the coast. Passed around more times than a peace pipe, and who knew what she'd contracted.

And he was trying to change his ways. Not to say that he was denying himself—he just wasn't overindulging.

He had behaved like a kid in a candy store when he'd first arrived. Errol had warned him to be careful, reminding him of the large number of HIV cases the island carried. And for once, Tony actually heeded his words and took it down two notches.

He wanted to be around for a long time. He wanted to enjoy the fruits of his labor, and how could he do that if he was dead?

CHAPTER

Forty-seven

Three weeks, two days, five hours, and twenty minutes later, Mildred was still convinced that they were trying to kill her. Or drive her insane!

Someone (she suspected Chevy) had snuck into her room and stolen her cell phone as well as her passport. When she reported the theft to the front desk, they said they would check into it and that in the meantime she could use the house phone to make a local call.

And with regards to her passport, well, she would have to go visit the American embassy for that.

And how the hell was she going to get there?

"Miss Cambridge can drive you in the hotel car."

"Yeah, right!"

And what she'd quickly realized after her first horrific

day was that all of the guests at the hotel were overweight and mostly women. But they of course were there of their own free will and couldn't understand why on her third day, during the morning run, Mildred had suddenly bolted off across the lawn toward the entrance gates.

"Didn't you know the gates had a low volt of electricity running through them? Just in case, you know, one of us wigs out in the middle of the program," explained a short Argentinean woman with the slight mustache who was leaning over the semiconscious Mildred.

Of course she didn't know that.

None of the articles she'd read about hotels ever talked about electrified fences!

"Read your manual, dear," the woman advised as the medics lifted Mildred onto the gurney.

Two Months and Counting . . .

✦

CHAPTER

Forty-eight

Countless attempts at escape later, Mildred finally surrendered to Miriam, Chevy, and the program.

By the first week in December, Mildred was fifty pounds lighter and Chevy said, "You look like a different person."

Even though Mildred's clothes hung limply from her body, whenever she looked in the mirror the same person she'd known her entire life looked back at her.

There was a beautician on the property, and Chevy had suggested she go.

"Why?" Mildred had whined.

"Because that ponytail is so tired, it's dead!"

Mildred succumbed, and when she emerged she had a new bronze hair color and a mass of shiny twists. She wasn't too happy about the new style. She thought it made her face look fat.

But then one day as she was sitting out in the garden, Mike, the hotel custodian, walked past her, doubled back, and announced with a big, broad grin on his face: "You look very nice today, Ms. Mildred."

Mildred looked over her shoulder. Surely he was referring to some other Mildred? But his eyes were locked on her, and then he winked before turning and walking away.

Mildred was stunned and she sat there on the lounge chair for a good twenty minutes before rushing off to her room and the mirror that hung on the wall. It was still Mildred looking back at her. She squinted and pushed her head closer to her image, looking deeper into the eyes that looked back at her.

She did kind of look cute, didn't she?

From then on, her confidence level began to rise. She made it a point to walk with her head up and back straight. And she'd also begun chanting to herself: "I am beautiful. I am gorgeous."

And damned if she didn't start to believe it!

Three weeks into her stay, she'd met Dr. Heath and had spent an entire evening listening to him explain, over dinner, the reason that Chimbarosa was run the way it was.

Gestapo-like.

"Most people want the best for themselves—really, they do—but we are human and we are fundamentally weak beings, failing time in and time out to achieve the thing we want most for ourselves."

Mildred didn't know if she believed in all of that, but she continued to listen.

"I want Chimbarosa to be a place to challenge that weak side. This particular property focuses on those with food issues." He paused then and stared at her over his wire-frame glasses. "People like yourself, Mildred."

Mildred had bristled at his comment but said nothing.

"When you walk out of here," he continued, "you'll walk out a new woman from the inside out."

Mildred supposed that that last statement was true, because upon his return two months later he was introducing himself to Mildred as if they'd never met.

Mildred took his hand in hers and said, "Dr. Heath, it's me. Mildred Johnson."

Dr. Heath's mouth dropped open and he took three steps backward. "You're not!"

Mildred blushed. "Yes, yes, I am."

"My God, you look fabulous!"

Mildred had never in her life been referred to as *fabulous* or any other adjective that would fall in the same category.

Mildred uttered a nervous "Thank you" as she fiddled with the bridge of her glasses.

"I don't think any of my guests have had the results you've achieved in such a short amount of time," Heath gushed. "I think you need to be our spokesperson!"

Surely he was kidding?

Wasn't a spokesperson something like a spokesmodel?

The word reverberated in her mind:

Model. Model. Model. Model.

Mildred gave her head a violent shake.

"Tell me, Mildred: did Chevy take any before pictures of you?"

This man was serious. Mildred slowly nodded.

"Good. I'm going to get on this right away." Dr. Heath's voice was filled with excitement.

"Congratulations, Mildred. You've found your better self."

✦

She wasn't thin by any means, but she was now a perfect size twelve. That was a long way from a size twenty-four.

And now Mildred found that she couldn't stop looking at her butt. She'd always had a butt—well, she'd had a double-wide trailer type of behind—but this new ass was round and tight and evidently mesmerizing, because the men who worked on the property couldn't seem to concentrate on their work whenever she was around.

And she had a walk too.

Well, that's what Chevy said.

A walk that had been hidden for years beneath the weight.

And Mildred had cheekbones! Native American type cheekbones. High and striking. And between the lack of junk food and the increase in her fruit, vegetable, and water consumption, her skin tone had taken on a healthy glow that was complemented by the suntan she sported.

She was feeling really good about herself. The best

she'd ever felt about herself, actually. Well, until she met with Chevy and Dr. Heath for her exit interview.

"Those tits! Those tits have got to go. They're like hot water bottles," Chevy said, pointing to them. "And those glasses . . . those awful glasses have got to go, as well!"

Mildred pushed her glasses back up her nose and then folded her arms protectively across her sagging breasts.

"Your breasts belong to the body you used to have," Dr. Heath explained. "And, well, it's 2007—I'm sure you're ready for contacts by now, hmmm?" Dr. Heath reached for Mildred's bifocals and removed them. "What big beautiful eyes you have, Mildred!"

Mildred blinked at Dr. Heath's blurry image before reaching for her glasses.

"Contacts are fine I suppose, but an operation?" she said after she'd put on her glasses.

Dr. Heath leaned forward and rested those fatherly eyes on Mildred. "It's a practically painless procedure."

"You said practically painless—" Mildred started.

"Aw, c'mon," Chevy erupted, banging her hands down on the table. "No pain, no fucking gain!"

Dr. Heath sighed. "Mildred, darling, there is absolutely nothing for you to worry about. I will handle the procedure myself." And then he looked calmly over at Chevy and said, "Dear, I think you need to take some time off."

CHAPTER

Forty-nine

It was just about eleven in the morning when the tourists started to slowly drift into the Blue Monkey Beach Bar and situate themselves at the umbrella-shaded tables, ordering the first of many rounds of beer, rum punch, or frosted fruity cocktails.

Tony was seated at a table right alongside the railing overlooking the beach, which allowed him a bird's-eye view of everything and everyone.

His Jet Skis had been in the water since ten o'clock, and from looking at his planner he saw that they were booked solid until three that afternoon.

"Can I get you something, Tony?" the pretty young waitress inquired.

Tony looked up at her. Her name was Ritz and she had

green eyes. She was a beauty, but a beauty that was too young for him. He'd heard from the other guys that she'd just made nineteen years old a few weeks back, even though she had the body of a twenty-five-year-old. He also knew that she'd been fucking since she was thirteen, which was probably why her body was so womanly.

"Just some water," Tony said, and then licked his lips as he watched the girl stroll off. He could kick himself for having morals, because he sure did want to hit that!

He turned his attention back to the beach. The chaise lounges the bar rented out were filling up quickly, and those who did not want a chaise lounge spread their blankets on the hot sand.

This was his favorite part of the day, when the European girls came down and dropped their tops to get an even tan. He was treated to the sight of rows and rows of perky nipples reaching toward the sun.

Ritz returned with the water and her number scribbled noticeably on the napkin. Tony smiled and nodded at her. He would keep the number, and maybe in a year or so . . .

Tony shook the thought off and crumpled the napkin into a ball. Just as he was about to take a swig of the water, he looked up and saw two women walking down the beach. One was dark-skinned with long black hair. She had on a wide-brimmed straw hat, dark shades, and a glaringly white one-piece bathing suit that left little to the imagination; so many critical panels had been excluded.

The woman who walked a little behind her was brown-skinned, with . . . Tony leaned forward and removed his shades . . . he couldn't tell if she had locks or braids. She wasn't as tall as the first woman, and the white cover-up she wore fell to her knees. Tony smirked. Well, at least from what he could see, she had nice calves.

✦

"You're being stupid."

"I'm not."

"You're going to sit out in this hot sun in that cover-up."

"It's not so hot."

"Take it off."

"I-I can't."

"If you don't, I will."

This was Mildred's second trip away from the Chimbarosa property. The first trip had been to Bridgetown, shopping for a new wardrobe. A lot of good it was going to do her; it was wintertime back in the States and there wasn't a turtleneck to be found in any one of the island shops.

She was scheduled to head back to New York in three days and so was trying to get in as many touristy activities as possible.

She'd begged Chevy to accompany her to the beach and Chevy had agreed, but not until she'd bitched and moaned about how much damage the sun did to one's skin.

Now, at Chevy's threat, Mildred took hold of the hem of the cover-up and began to slowly raise it. When it got to her waist, she chickened out and dropped it back down to her knees again.

Chevy gave her an icy look.

"Okay, damn," Mildred said, and in one quick move she disrobed and then quickly sat down on the chaise.

She was waiting for the entire beach to erupt in laughter, but all she heard was an approving whistle.

"See?" Chevy grinned.

◆

She'd moved quick, but Tony did catch a glance, and he liked what he saw. "Damn," he muttered to himself as he stood up and started down the steps and across the sand toward the two women.

"I'm thirsty," Chevy uttered casually. "Why don't you go get us a cold drink?"

Mildred sighed. What, now she was her maid too?

"Up there, at the bar," Chevy said, lifting her hand and pointing toward the restaurant.

Mildred squinted. The sun reflected off the sand, blinding her. Turning around, she reached for her cover-up and found that it was gone.

"Chevy?"

"What?"

"Where is it?"

"Where's what?"

Mildred was exasperated. "I know you don't expect me to walk up there in just my bathing suit."

Chevy ignored her as she smeared sunblock down her arm.

"Well, I guess you won't be getting your cool drink then, 'cause I ain't going without my cover-up."

Mildred flopped back down into her chair.

"Oh, all right, you big baby!" Chevy reached into her straw bag, pulled out the cover-up, and tossed it at Mildred. "Now go!"

Mildred was proud of herself. It was rare that she won a round with Chevy.

Now standing up again, she slipped the cover-up over her head, and when she looked up, she saw someone that stopped her heart.

Mildred blinked, rubbed her eyes, and then blinked again. She was still getting used to wearing contacts.

"Oh, shit," she whispered.

"What?" Chevy said, sitting up and looking in the direction Mildred was fixated on.

"That's . . . that's . . ." Mildred stuttered. Her entire body began to shake.

"That's who?" Chevy asked, and then looked at Mildred's trembling flesh. "What the hell is wrong with you, girl?"

"It's him," Mildred said in a quivering voice.

"Him who?" Chevy gave Mildred's thigh a sharp slap.

"Tony," Mildred whispered in disbelief.

Chevy's neck snapped and her head swung around again.

"Tony from New York Tony?"

Mildred slowly nodded.

"Are you sure?"

Again Mildred nodded her head.

Tony had on his Hollywood smile, the smile he was wearing the very first time Mildred had laid eyes on him. It was like déjà vu.

She watched in quiet amazement as he approached. Strong thighs cooked a deep chocolate brown from the sun. Biceps more muscular than she remembered, and of course there was the ever-present bulge.

Mildred felt as if she was about to faint and grabbed hold of the chair, steadying herself.

"Hello," Tony said when he was just a foot away. "I'm Tony. I just had to come over and introduce myself to you gorgeous women."

His eyes were glued to Mildred and he gave her an appreciative nod.

Both Chevy and Mildred were struck speechless.

Silence hung between them. Silence so long that time itself seemed to have come to a halt. And in that moment Mildred recalled with vivid clarity every single word that had passed between them. She relived every sexual encounter and then that awful day when she, dressed in her wedding gown, realized that she had been taken for a fool.

She'd thought she'd rid herself of the anger the way she'd rid herself of the weight, but in that moment she knew that it was still there, and growing with every breath she took.

Finally, Chevy broke the trance.

"I'm Chevanese Cambridge. But everybody calls me Chevy," Chevy said, extending her hand to him. Tony shook it, his eyes still glued to Mildred.

"And you are?" Tony asked, holding his hand out to Mildred.

Mildred couldn't believe it. He didn't recognize her. He really didn't recognize her!

She didn't know what to say, how to respond. Her mouth was working, but nothing came out.

So Chevy jumped in and said, "Oh, this is M—"

At that moment, Mildred sprang to life.

"I'm Karma," she said.

Tony took her hand into his. "Karma? What a unique and beautiful name."

Mildred had to force a smile. His touch made her skin crawl.

"I've never seen you girls here before. Did you just fly in?"

Again Chevy opened her mouth to answer but was blocked by Mildred's quick response.

"I came in last night to visit Chevy . . . She lives here."

"First time on the island?"

Mildred nodded.

"It's a lovely place to visit, an even better place to live," Tony said.

Chevy realized that he was still holding Mildred's hand.

"Really?" Mildred said. "Do you live here?"

"Well, now I do," Tony said. "I'm building a house just up the road from here."

Mildred felt her insides turn over.

With the money I helped you steal!

"That's nice," Chevy interjected. "So, what kind of work do you do?"

Tony finally turned his attention to Chevy. "A little bit of this and a little bit of that."

Releasing Mildred's hand, he pointed out to the ocean.

"You see those two Jet Skis, the ones with the yellow, green, and black stripes?"

Chevy and Mildred turned and peered out at the ocean.

"I rent those out to the tourists," he proudly announced, "but I'd be willing to take you ladies out for a ride at no charge."

Chevy knew the offer was really meant for Mildred.

"I'd like that," Mildred said in a confident voice. "I'd like that very much."

Tony pulled a business card from the back pocket of his swim trunks and handed it to Mildred.

"I'll be waiting for your call," he said before flashing his million-dollar smile and strutting off.

Mildred imagined herself leaping on top of him and driving punch after punch into his head before stomping him into the sand.

"Well, Miss Thang," Chevy sang. "Or shall I refer to you as Karma?"

Mildred said nothing.

"The universe can be a strange and wonderful place," Chevy mused aloud.

"How so?"

"Look, it placed you two at the same company in New

York and now on the same island. Don't you find that strange?"

Mildred found it disturbing.

"Well, I guess we should get going, huh? You've got to get back, start packing—"

"Oh, no. I'm not going no-fucking-where," Mildred emphatically announced. "Not until I ruin him."

Chevy felt a cold shiver shoot down her spine. She didn't think Geneva knew all of what went on between those two, but Chevy had the distinct feeling that it constituted more than a broken heart.

◆

Tony sent two rum punches over to the women. And though he didn't approach them again for the rest of the time they were there, he did spy from behind the safety of his sunglasses.

He couldn't shake the feeling that there was something terribly familiar about that Karma woman. Something he couldn't put his finger on. Something that made his balls tingle. His balls were never wrong, but shit, she was gorgeous and he just wouldn't be Tony Landry if he didn't go for it—tingling balls or no tingling balls—now would he?

CHAPTER

Fifty

You've got to be kidding me," Geneva wailed from her bedroom in Manhattan. "He's there?"

Mildred clutched the phone tightly in her hand.

"Yes. I don't believe it myself."

"And are you sure he didn't recognize you?"

"I'm sure."

"Do you really look that much different?" Geneva's tone was skeptical.

"I guess. I must—he stood a foot away from me and I didn't see a flicker of recognition on his face." Mildred sounded unsure. "Well, you decide," she continued, and used the cell phone to snap a picture of herself. "I'm sending you a picture to your cell."

Geneva was quiet for a while, and then Mildred heard a beeping sound coming from Geneva's end of the line. "Just a second," Geneva said, and then off in the distance Mildred could hear her howl, "Holy fucking shit!" and then into the phone, "Y'all think I'm stupid, don't you?"

"Geneva, what—?"

"Did Chevy put you up to this?"

"Chevy? No, I—"

"There is no way in the world that this is you, Mildred. In fact, is this even Mildred that I'm speaking to? 'Cause if you want to know the truth, it don't really sound like you."

Well, she knew she sounded a little different. She was certainly more confident; she was sure that was apparent, even in her voice.

But still, Mildred felt insulted. Had she been that horrible a sight before?

"Geneva!" Mildred yelled into the phone. "It's me. I swear on my mother's grave, it's me!"

Geneva went quiet again. To tell the truth, she was a little envious. She took control of her emotions and said, "For real?"

"Yes, for real."

"Well, girl, you look good. Damn good."

"Thank you."

"But you're not going to call him, are you?"

Mildred's eyes popped. Of course she was going to call him.

"Well, I had intended to—"

Geneva's voice climbed. "After what he did to you,

why in the world would you want to give that bastard even an ounce of your time!"

Mildred allowed Geneva to rant for another few seconds before cutting her off.

"It's not what you think, Geneva."

"What is it, then?"

Geneva suddenly felt a pang of horror resound through her.

"Now wait a minute, Mildred, you're not intending to . . . I mean, you're not going to—"

"Kill him?"

Mildred's tone was like ice.

Geneva was almost afraid to ask: "Are you?"

Mildred was silent for a moment. She'd imagined killing him a number of different times in just as many ways. But death was too easy a punishment. Tony needed to suffer.

"No. That is not my intention."

"Then what are you planning on doing?"

"I think the less you know, the better, Geneva."

Geneva pulled the phone away from her ear and stared at it in utter amazement. Was this her mild-mannered friend Mildred Johnson?

"What has Chevy done to you?"

Mildred thought about that for a moment. "I guess," she said in a chilling tone, "something that I wouldn't have been able to do for myself."

Geneva didn't quite understand her response.

"Mildred—"

"Geneva, I gotta go. I'll call you in a week."

CHAPTER

Fifty-one

Three days later, Mildred dialed Tony's number.

"Hi, Tony this is Mil—I mean, Karma."

Tony was in bed. He turned over onto his side and raised himself up on one elbow.

Tony grinned. He knew she'd call, even if it did take three days. They always called.

"Hey, how are you?"

"I'm well, and yourself?"

"Couldn't be better."

Tony was good at the small talk. He knew how to make women feel comfortable, how to make them feel safe.

After a few minutes of this it was Mildred who lunged forward and said, "I'd really like to see you again."

Tony wasn't surprised. They all wanted to see him . . . again.

"Sure. How does tomorrow evening sound?"

"Tomorrow will be fine."

"I'll pick you up—"

"No, that's okay. I'll meet you. Just tell me where."

Tony's mind raced for a minute. Tomorrow was Sunday night. He knew the perfect place.

"Okay, meet me at Tam's Wok on First Street in Holetown."

"Will do," Mildred said.

Tony flipped his phone closed and then turned to look at the beauty that was currently splayed out naked beside him.

"Who was that?" the woman asked, flipping her blond hair away from her eyes.

"My mother." Tony's response was nonchalant as he reached over and pulled her on top of him.

"Didn't sound like any conversation I've ever heard a man have with his mother," she remarked in her British tongue.

Tony grunted, slapped her on the ass, and said, "Are we here to dissect my conversations, or are we here to fuck?"

The woman, Tony couldn't quite remember her name. He thought it was Ginger or Ginseng . . . something like that. But it didn't matter—she was flying out that evening and he was sure he would never see her again.

"I like it from behind," she purred into his ear.

Fine by him! Tony hastily flipped her onto her belly and mounted her from behind.

"I like it rough," she called to him over her shoulder.

"As you wish!" Tony laughed as he gripped her hips and jerked her roughly up onto her knees.

He rolled the condom onto his penis and was about to enter her when she pulled away.

"What?"

"I like it in my ass," she said coyly as she batted her fake eyelashes at him.

Tony grinned; he liked it there too.

He stuck four fingers of his left hand into his mouth, then pulled them out and ran them down the center of Ginger's crack, moistening her exit way. Ginger moaned and flung her long blond hair over her shoulder. "Grab my hair," she said, and Tony did. Took hold of it the way a cowboy would take hold of his mare's reins.

He slowly glided the tip of his dick into her anus. It was tight, and the pleasure was immediate. Before he knew it he was completely in, stroking as easily as if he'd entered her missionary-style.

Ginger screamed, "Deeper, harder, faster!"

And Tony wrapped his hands tighter around her mane of hair and began to oblige.

✦

Sunday night was karaoke night on First Street, and the street came alive with partygoers, like a scaled-down version of the famous Memphis Beale Street.

Tam's Wok, a Chinese Thai restaurant, was located directly across from the karaoke tent. When Tony made the dinner reservations, he specifically requested that he and his date be seated on the outside terrace, which overlooked the bustling sidewalk.

Mildred had piled her twists high on her head and clasped her hair with an ornately decorated mocha-colored band. She'd chosen a long pale blue linen tube dress that hugged her curvaceous figure like a second skin. When she climbed into the backseat of the taxi, the driver gave her an approving glance in the rearview mirror and said, "What a lucky man."

Mildred had been lost in her thoughts. " 'Scuse me?"

"I said, what a lucky man."

Mildred was confused. "Who?"

"Why, your husband, of course!"

"No, I'm not married."

"Well, then, your boyfriend?"

Mildred shook her head.

The man smiled so broadly that his white teeth filled the rearview mirror.

"Well, I'm free and single myself . . ."

Mildred half listened as the man droned on and on about how he could make her happy and how he would love her like no other.

Ever since she'd lost the weight and had the boob job done, it'd been one man after the other making passes at her. At first she had to admit that she was flattered, but after a few weeks she began to become tired of the attention and then annoyed.

"I'm gay," Mildred announced drily.

The driver gave her one last pitiful look and then said no more.

It took less than twenty minutes to get to Holetown. Earlier that day she'd felt nervous about the date, snatching up the phone on more than one occasion to call Tony and cancel. But then she'd think back on all of the pain, suffering, and humiliation he'd caused her and find strength again.

A devious smile flashed across her face as she envisioned herself smiling sweetly across the table at him before yelling out her real name and then plunging the butter knife into his chest.

"Fifteen dollars," the driver said without looking at her.

Mildred handed him a twenty, adjusted her dress, and started toward the restaurant.

Heads turned as she snaked slowly through the crowd. Women threw her nasty looks while the men slowly undressed her in their minds.

She ignored the few who had the nerve to approach her.

"Karma," Tony sang, his face bright with approval. "You look beautiful."

"Thank you." Karma smiled back. "And you look very handsome."

Tony had donned a white pair of chinos and a black silk T-shirt.

He thanked her and pulled the door open.

Seated at their table, the conversation was bumpy at first, because Mildred still couldn't believe that he didn't recognize her. Finally she fell into a familiar groove and began to engage him the way she had when she thought he really loved her. After that, the conversation flowed as smooth as cream.

Mildred hadn't even thought of a backstory, but the fantastical lie spilled out of her as if it'd been rehearsed a million times:

Karma Jackson was the daughter of wealthy parents who didn't understand her. A Barnard graduate. Five years with the Metropolitan Museum of Art. Then off to Princeton for her master's.

After that, a year abroad.

Where?

Why, Europe, of course!

Did she have a boyfriend?

Well, no, she didn't. In fact, she'd had only one boy-friend in her entire life—a man she thought she would marry, but he'd broken her heart.

Tony took her hand; he was sorry. Sometimes bad things happen to good people. But that man's irresponsibil-ity was his good luck, because she was there with him now.

What are your aspirations?

Marriage. Family. Happiness.

Me too.

✦

In between the getting-to-know-you stuff, Karma laughed until tears spilled from her eyes at the horrible karaoke contestants.

Tony liked her laugh.

They got up from the table when the island's most popular karaoke singer jumped up onto the stage: Gabriele, a long, lanky, damn near toothless Rastafarian.

The audience erupted in applause, not because he could sing but because he was horrible. Horrible to the point that people pressed their hands to their ears and scrunched their faces in pain. Even so, they begged for more, because Gabriele had heart and he had character and was apparently oblivious to the fact that he couldn't sing.

Mildred laughed until a realization smacked her squarely in the face, and then she was suddenly serious.

She and Gabriele were very much alike.

"What's wrong?"

Mildred snapped back. "Oh, nothing—just zoned out for a minute."

They went down to the street and moved close to the stage to watch a white man belt out Gloria Gaynor's "I Will Survive."

"Why don't you go on up there? You look like you have a pretty good set of lungs on you."

Tony's eyes slid over Mildred's perky breasts before climbing her neck and resting on her face.

"Nah." She waved her hand. "I can't sing."

Tony pointed at the person who was currently bouncing across the stage singing the Stevie Wonder classic "Do I Do." "And he can?"

Mildred laughed. Yeah, this guy was even worse than Gabriele.

"C'mon, go ahead." Tony nudged her gently.

"Why don't you?"

Tony raised his hands. "Are you crazy? I live here. You, on the other hand, are just here on vacation."

Mildred nodded.

Why the hell not?

"Okay, I'll do it."

Together they walked to the side of the stage and flipped through the massive leather-bound songbooks.

"Oh, I see one," Mildred chirped, snapping the book shut before Tony could see it.

She signed her name to the list and found that she could barely contain herself as she waited through the two people ahead of her.

"So here now we got Karma Jackson coming up to the mike to sing that famous Rick James and Tina Marie love song, 'Fire and Desire'!"

Mildred walked nervously to the microphone, tapped it twice, and then nodded her head that she was ready to begin. When the musical introduction began, Mildred realized to her horror that she'd have to sing both parts—male and female.

Just as Rick James began his monologue, Gabriele appeared and slid across the stage on his knees, coming to dramatic stop at Mildred's feet.

The crowd exploded as he croaked through the Rick James portion of the song.

Mildred didn't consider herself a singer, but she could hold a note with the best of them, and when the Tina Marie part came up, Mildred threw her hands into the air and gave it all she had.

Tony, who'd been leaning up against a light pole talking to a friend of his, was stunned, and he began to applaud loudly.

Mildred belted out passionate line after passionate line, and at some point she would swear she felt her body and soul separate, and when they joined together again, she felt less like Mildred Johnson and more like Karma Jackson.

Toward the end of the song, she found Tony's face in the crowd, and he was looking at her in a way he never had when she was Mildred Johnson.

Fifty-two

Errol listened as Tony rambled on and on about this new woman he'd met. He couldn't remember a time when Tony had sounded this excited about a woman.

"And her real name is Karma?"

"Yeah, I know. It's an odd name, but it fits her, it really does."

"How so?"

"I don't know how to explain it. I mean, she's gorgeous and she's got this great spirit . . . she's just perfect."

Errol pulled the phone away from his face and stared at it. He could swear, just from the sound of Tony's voice, that he was swooning on the other end.

"Damn, all of this after just one date? Sounds to me like you're whipped, and she ain't even give you none yet!"

Tony laughed and waved his hand in the air. "C'mon, man. It ain't nothing like that."

"Sounds like everything like that."

"Whatever, dude. So when you coming down?"

"My secretary is making the arrangements, so I'll let you know when I know."

"Cool."

"So how's your moms doing?"

Tony didn't really know. He hadn't spoken to her in weeks.

"She's all right," he lied.

Errol shook his head.

"You know," Errol carefully ventured, "there's a saying—"

"Oh, here we go!"

"Now, just humor me for a minute . . . There's an old saying that goes, 'See how a man treats his mother, and know how you too will be treated,' and I'm paraphrasing here."

Tony jumped to the defensive. "What are you trying to say, Errol?"

"I think you know."

"Yeah, whatever. I gotta go."

"*Ciao.*"

Tony wasn't going to let Errol kill his good mood with all his righteous bullshit. He would call his mother as soon as he had time.

Fifty-three

What the hell are these?" Mildred stared curiously down at the pair of small gray metal balls Chevy held in her hand.

"Kegel balls."

"Kegel balls? What the hell is that?"

"They're used to tighten your vagina muscles."

Mildred just stared at her. "And?"

"And"—Chevy took a step closer to Mildred, bringing the balls eye level to Mildred's face—"it can't hurt."

Mildred was still confused.

"Can't hurt what?"

Mildred could be so exasperating. "It can't hurt that when you finally fuck him, you'll be able to squeeze the hell out of his dick and give him the most explosive orgasm he's ever fucking had," Chevy calmly advised.

Mildred's eyes popped.

Chevy gave her a sly look.

"Isn't that the way he got you, Mildred?" Chevy started walking an ominous circle around her as she rolled the Kegel balls in her hand. "He used his good looks, his charm, and his . . . sex?"

In actuality he'd had her at hello . . . but Chevy did have a point.

"It's obvious that he likes you. How many times has he called since you two went out?"

"Four."

"And that's just been in two days. At least we know he's interested."

Mildred nodded.

"This needs to be a systematic undoing. Break him down layer by cruddy layer until he is . . . well, what you were when you arrived at Chimbarosa," Chevy said as she pressed the balls into Mildred's hand.

Mildred gave the balls a doubtful look. "How do I use them?"

"Well, my dear," Chevy began, a mischievous smile on her face, "you just insert them up inside you and hold them there."

◆

Mildred sat on her bed for an hour, staring at the balls. She couldn't believe what her life had suddenly come to.

How did I arrive at this point? she asked herself as she rolled the steel balls round and round her palm.

She raised her sundress and slowly slipped off her thong. Lying down on the bed, she slipped one ball up inside her and then the other.

She lay there for a minute, allowing herself to become accustomed to the foreign objects in her body.

After a while, she slowly slipped off the bed. She stood, her legs pressed tightly together as she contracted and released her vagina muscles. Giggling, she realized she was actually getting a little thrill.

Contract.

Release.

Contract.

Release.

She began snapping her fingers to the rhythm.

Contract.

Release.

A knock came at the door. "Ms. Mildred?"

Mildred froze. "Yes?"

"It's Mike from maintenance. I understand you have a problem with your toilet?"

"Oh, yes," Mildred said, and sat down on the bed. "Come in."

Mike pushed the door open and walked in. Today he was dressed in a clean white sleeveless T-shirt and his blue work pants. His muscles rippled as he shifted his tool bag from one hand to the other.

"Hello, Ms. Mildred," he said, and gave her a shy smile.

They had been engaged in a light flirtation ever since

he'd given her that compliment. Now, as he stood there before her, Mildred felt herself starting to become excited.

"Hello, Mike," she said.

"You're looking very nice today, Ms. Mildred," he said, his eyes undressing her.

Mildred blushed, casually crossed her legs, and said, "Thank you."

They stared at each other for a long moment before Mike cleared his throat and said, "What can I do for you today?"

Mildred had a few suggestions. First he could strip out of those clothes and then he could put his dick right in her hot, throbbing . . .

Mildred shook the thought away.

"Oh, um, the toilet . . . it's just not flushing right," Mildred responded in a small voice.

Had it gotten warmer in the room since he'd walked in? She thought it had, because she had a line of perspiration across the top of her lip.

"Okay," Mike said, and started toward the bathroom.

Mildred watched him go and then suddenly realized that she had some of her intimates drying on the shower curtain pole. That's not anything she needed him to see.

"Oh, wait a minute," she blurted, jumping up and making a mad dash into the bathroom.

Mike waited patiently as he observed the black net thong that had been forgotten in the middle of the floor.

Mildred reentered, two pairs of panties balled safely in her fists. Mike smiled slyly at her and then nodded at the forgotten undies on the floor.

Mortified, Mildred bent over and snatched them up. When she was upright again, she had a sheepish grin on her face. "Sorry," she muttered.

"No problem," he said as he looked deep into her eyes. He started to turn around and then turned back to face her again. "Ms. Mildred, I—"

Mildred grabbed hold of him and pressed her mouth against his. The tool bag clanged noisily to the floor as a surprised Mike wrapped his arms around her waist and pulled him to her.

Their tongues probed hungrily in each other's mouths and Mildred's knees went weak when she felt Mike's cock push eagerly against her thigh.

What am I doing? she thought as they clung to each other and awkwardly stumbled toward the bed.

Mike quickly pulled his shirt over his head and tossed it to the floor as Mildred feverishly worked at pulling off her sundress. She had it halfway up when the unthinkable occurred.

Clump, clump.

Mildred looked down and could have melted away with shame. She'd forgotten about the Kegel balls, and now there they were on the floor, gleaming with her juices, rolling slowly between Mike's feet.

Mike watched them in amazement. "Did those just come out of you?"

Mildred dropped her eyes and nodded in embarrassment. When she raised her eyes again, she knew their time had passed. The moment was gone.

"Well," Mike said, diverting his eyes to the wall and

scratching the back of his neck, "I guess I'll be getting to that toilet," he said.

"Yeah, yeah," Mildred mumbled.

Mike retrieved his shirt and tool bag and walked into the bathroom mumbling something about strange Yankee women.

CHAPTER

Fifty-four

It was a cute house.

The outside was painted a warm coconut color, and the windows had white shutters. The front yard was filled with foliage and the tiled veranda had potted plants in each corner as well as two wicker chairs.

"Nice," Mildred commented as she followed Tony around to the side door.

Walking inside, they first came upon a dining table. To the right of that there was a small sofa that faced the back of the house and the sliding glass doors that led out to the veranda.

"Welcome to my home," Tony said as he led her toward the couch.

Against the wall was a small stereo system.

As if reading her mind, Tony said, "The television is in the bedroom."

Tony was nervous. He couldn't remember a time when he'd ever been nervous about having a woman over. He'd spent all morning cleaning and then most of the afternoon trying to figure out what it was he was going to wear.

"Please sit," he said. "Can I get you something to drink? Coffee, water . . ."

"How about a glass of wine?"

"White or red?" he called out to her as he disappeared down the hall to the kitchen.

"White is fine."

Smooth jazz sailed from the stereo as they sat sipping their wine. Mildred could see Tony watching her from the corner of his eye, although she pretended to be completely engrossed on the view outside the glass doors.

They were supposed to go down to Coach House, a popular restaurant and bar. A local band was playing there tonight, and Tony felt that that would be the perfect opportunity to get a bit closer to Karma.

Dancing always broke the ice.

"Are you okay?"

"Yeah, why?" Tony said, clearing his throat.

Mildred rolled the stem of the glass between her fingers. "I don't know—you looked like your mind was a million miles away."

His mind wasn't away; it was right there in that house, with her.

"Did I tell you you're looking really beautiful tonight?"

Mildred nodded.

He had told her, twice.

At Chevy's insistence, she wore a peach-colored spaghetti-strapped dress that fell just below the knee. Around her neck was a large iridescent angel shell on a thin leather string. Her hair was out, but brushed away from her face, exposing the large wooden hoop earrings she wore.

She had on a little mascara and Oh Baby Mac lip gloss that brought out the sun-kissed tone of her skin.

"Yes, you did, and thank you again."

Tony inched a little bit closer to her. "You smell wonderful. What's that you're wearing?"

Mildred wasn't surprised to feel a wave of warmth roll through her midsection coming to settle in between her thighs. She'd be a liar if she said she no longer had feelings for him, because she did. Feelings like that don't die so easy. But she despised him too, and that was the emotion she forced her mind to concentrate on.

"Oh, look at the time," she blurted suddenly, jumping up from the couch.

Tony sighed. "Yeah, I think we should get going."

◆

The Coach House, like so many other establishments on the island, had once been the home of a reputable doctor, but more than twenty years ago it had been turned into a bar and restaurant, offering open-air dining beneath the stars. The bar area was a popular gathering spot for locals, expats, and tourists, who threw back drink after drink as they watched cricket and soccer matches on the forty-inch flat-screen television. There was a pool table beyond the bar, and on Thursday nights a local band, along with half-priced drinks, brought in hundreds of people from all over the tiny island.

Tony and Mildred took a seat beside a palm tree with its trunk twined in clear Christmas lights.

"I'll have the pumpkin soup and the house salad," Mildred said, handing her menu to the waiter.

"And you, sir?"

"Um, give me the grilled snapper with plantains and salad."

When the waiter hurried off to fill their orders, Tony lifted his glass of champagne in the air.

"To you."

A blushing Mildred reached for her own glass. "Thank you."

Their glasses came together.

Mildred's head was light. She'd only had breakfast that morning, and now the glass of wine she'd consumed at Tony's place and this champagne were making her feel giddy.

Tony was gazing at her, the reflection of the small tea candle flame dancing in his irises.

"What?" Mildred asked in a demure voice.

"I don't know," Tony said, shaking his head in bewilderment. "There's something about you that I just can't put my finger on."

Mildred's heart began to race. Was he beginning to realize who she was? Panicked, she reached for her glass and drained its contents.

"Easy with that." Tony laughed, reaching for the champagne bottle and filling Mildred's glass.

Mildred shot him an embarrassed grin.

"Don't get me wrong, it's a good thing. It feels familiar."

"Familiar?" Mildred's eyes bulged.

"Yeah," Tony said, reaching across the table and taking her hand in his. "It's like I've known you my entire life," he said as his thumb moved seductively over the back of her hand.

Small electric jolts shot through Mildred.

"Maybe in a past life?"

Tony laughed. "Maybe that's it!"

✦

After their meal, Tony suggested a game of pool.

"I don't know how to play."

"Don't worry; I'll teach you."

Mildred was feeling so mellow, her eyes were droopy and she couldn't get rid of the mischievous grin stuck as if with glue on her face.

"You're even sexier when you're drunk," Tony whispered in her ear.

"I-I'm not drunk!" Mildred laughed.

Tony stood behind her. "Okay, sure," he said in a patronizing tone. "Now, this is how you hold the cue stick."

"Oh, I see."

"Now bend," Tony instructed.

Mildred bent over and her body took on a seductive curve. "Like this?"

Tony could feel his dick stiffening as he gazed down at Mildred's plump behind. Maybe this wasn't such a good idea.

"Like this, Tony?" she repeated when he didn't respond.

"Yeah, baby, just like that!" yelled out a man who'd also been ogling her behind, from the bar.

Tony turned cold eyes on him but said nothing.

"Karma, you don't have to bend over quite so far," he said, suddenly feeling very possessive.

Another bottle of champagne and two really bad games of pool later, they found themselves stumbling down the road toward Tony's house. The alcohol had swelled Mildred's feet something awful, and she'd slipped out of her high heels.

"Here," she slurred in a demanding tone, tossing the shoes at Tony, "carry these."

Tony, who was slightly less inebriated but inebriated just the same, barely caught hold of the shoes and then found himself slightly annoyed at her tone.

"What's the magic word?" he called to her.

Mildred turned on her bare heels and strutted provocatively toward him. As she approached, Tony could feel his balls begin to tingle. Looking closer, he saw a glint in Mildred's eyes that he hadn't noticed before.

Coming toward him, Mildred saw herself snatching the

stilettos from him and mashing one heel and then the next into each of his eyes.

When she was face-to-face with him, she raised her arms and was amused to see Tony cringe.

"Oh, *pleaaasee*," she cried, throwing her arms around him, leaning in to press her lips to his, instantly sweeping away the creepy feeling that had gripped him seconds earlier.

They strolled side by side toward Tony's rented house, Mildred's shoes dangling from Tony's hand by their straps. He mused that if one of his boys were there to witness the scene, they would certainly assume he was whipped. What was next, his carrying her pocketbook?

Closer to the house, Mildred threw her head back. "Oh, God—look at that moon!"

It was a beautiful sight: large, round, and bright.

"It's romantic, isn't it?" Tony said as he tilted his head back to admire it.

"Very."

"How about a walk on the beach?"

Tony removed his sandals and tossed their shoes inside the hull of a wooden fishing boat that had been pulled up and onto the beach. "It'll be safe, don't worry," Tony assured her when he saw the look of concern on her face.

The sand was soft beneath their feet as they strolled along in silence, hands linked, the sound of surf lapping gently against the shore in the background.

How many times had she fantasized about this exact moment? Too many to count, she mused as they walked along. And now there she was. The moment was so perfect, it was such a shame that it was happening with a lowdown backstabbing stuck-up son of a—

"Karma?"

Mildred snapped back.

"Wow, now whose mind is a million miles away?" Tony asked, his face glowing with amusement. "I called your name like three times."

"Oh," Mildred said with a wave of her hand, "I was just thinking what a beautiful night it is."

"That it is," Tony agreed, and with that he turned, swept her into his arms, and planted a passionate kiss on her lips.

Mildred, taken off-guard, made a weak attempt to push him away, but when his tongue found hers, she felt her legs go limp.

They kissed that way for some time, their hands moving slowly over each other's body. When the kiss finally came to an end, they remained pressed against each other, breathless with desire.

"I want you, Karma. I want you so bad," Tony unbelievingly heard himself utter.

Mildred was on fire. She pulled his lips back to hers as she reached down and caught hold of his shirt.

"What are you doing?" Tony asked when she'd raised the shirt up to his chest.

"Sssh." Mildred pressed her index finger gently against his lips. Tony fell quiet and allowed her to slowly undress him.

She held his gaze as she undid his zipper, slipped her hand inside his khakis, and found his throbbing member. Butterflies erupted in her stomach and a small sigh escaped her.

In her mind, she could clearly picture his penis—every bulging vein, its smooth, shiny tip. God, how she'd missed it.

"Hey, hey, let's go back to the house," Tony suggested when he thought he saw movement from behind a cluster of bearded fig trees. "Someone might see."

"I don't care who sees," Mildred said as she pulled his penis from his pants.

Mildred eased herself down onto the sand. Placing Tony's shirt beneath her head, she beckoned him with her eyes.

Tony climbed on top of her, hastily pushing his pants down and around his knees. They kissed passionately as he worked to remove first one breast and then the other from the bodice of her dress, after which he pressed them together, enclosing his mouth hungrily over both nipples, causing Mildred to cry out in pleasure.

As his tongue worked, something struck in him as he slowly realized that this was only the second woman he'd run across with such long, taut nipples. The first had been Mildred.

"Touch me," Mildred moaned into his ear as she guided his hand down between her legs. He worked his fingers beneath the silky strip of thong and was greeted with warm, sticky wetness.

His breathing became shallow as the excitement built. Mildred assisted in getting her thong off by shimmying her behind deep into the sand. The friction lent more heat to the already raging inferno inside of him.

Without even a thought of a condom, Tony pushed in.

Inhaling deeply, he took a moment to bask in the burning heat of her vagina before he pushed deeper.

"Oh, God," Mildred cried, clawing at his back.

"You can call me Tony," he said with a shuddering breath as he began the first of a series of rhythmic thrusts.

✦

"Yah nasty dog!"

Tony heard the damning words through the darkness. And then his foot was being kicked. His eyes flew open.

"Get up, yah nasty buzzard!"

Another kick was levied, this time to his thigh.

Baffled and confused, he bolted upright, rubbing his eyes and then peering at the person screaming at him.

He knew the face—her name was Anita and she sold fish at the fish stand located a few yards down the beach.

Tony's head pounded.

"Drunkard!" she spat.

What is this woman doing in his house?

"Murder! Murder!" the woman wailed as she started past him.

It was then that Tony realized he wasn't in his house but on the beach. In front of him, the sun was just peeking over the horizon. A few feet away a group of fishermen pointed and laughed as they hauled their boat into the water.

Tony looked down and his Johnson looked back at him. He was stark naked!

"Murder, murder!" the old woman continued to yell as she ran toward the road.

Yelling murder was the Bajan equivalent of yelling for help.

Tony jumped up and looked around wildly for his clothes. They were gone. Covering his penis, he ran down the beach, cutting up and between two clapboard houses before darting across the road (nearly getting hit by a speeding cement truck) and then onto the veranda of his house.

CHAPTER

Fifty-five

Chevy was laughing so hard, tears had started to drip from her eyes. "Are you serious?" she asked for the fifth time.

They were seated out on the terrace of her room. Mildred's legs were crossed and glistening in the sun.

"You fucked him and then you left him there on the beach? Naked? You took his clothes? You did all that?"

Mildred nodded and gave Chevy a mischievous grin.

Chevy raised her hand. "My girl!"

Mildred smacked her palm with her own.

"Did he call?"

Mildred nodded.

"Oooh, he's mad, ain't he?" Chevy leaned in. She was so enjoying this.

"Well, in the first message he sounded calm, but by message number five he was screaming like a—"

"Bitch?"

"Well, I was going to say like a banshee, but I guess *bitch* is just as good." Mildred laughed and they slapped palms again.

"Thank goodness he doesn't know where you're staying," Chevy said before turning her attention to a small yellow-bellied bird that had landed on the rim of the terrace, watching them curiously. "Well, if he still wants you after something like that, then I'd have to say that he's whipped and good."

"We'll see," Mildred said as she absentmindedly twirled a lock of hair between her fingers.

"So how are you going to explain yourself when you finally do speak to him?"

"I don't know. I haven't figured that out yet."

CHAPTER

Fifty-six

Tony's emotions and thoughts had run the gamut from anger to fear and back again.

They'd both been so drunk that it was a possibility that Karma had stumbled into the ocean and drowned. He'd gone back to the beach to see if he could find any evidence of that, but he was no policeman and he didn't know what to look for.

He'd called her cell phone numerous times, but the calls had gone directly to voice mail.

She could have wandered into the ocean, he thought again as he gazed out at the vast blue water.

"Nah," he muttered as he shook the terrible thought from his mind.

But what had happened to his clothes?

Maybe she took them?

But why would she?

Maybe someone had kidnapped her? There were sick people in the world. He imagined Karma tied up and naked in some filthy backroom, her assailant holding her as his personal sex slave.

"You're losing it, man!" Tony yelled out, and then quickly tried to erase the vision from his mind.

Sex slave?

He was too distraught and confused to even put his Jet Skis in the water that day. Instead, he spent the entire day with the phone book open on his lap as he called one hotel after the other in search of his mystery woman.

"May I speak to Karma Jackson, please?"

And with each call he received the same response: "Sorry, sir. We don't have a guest registered here with that name."

Tony walked circles as he scratched his head. None of it made sense. And to make things worse he hadn't used a condom! He didn't know this woman from Adam and he'd had unprotected sex with her.

Granted, it was probably the best sex he'd ever had. Just thinking about it caused his dick to react.

He wondered if he should call the police and report her missing, but he decided against it. The last thing he needed was to have an officer of the law snooping into his background. But if someone came to look for her, questions would be asked, and people had seen them together.

Tony's mind whirled. He tried Karma's cell again. Still no answer.

"Karma, please call me. I need to know that you're okay."

✦

Three days went by before Karma called.

Chevy had driven by his house and saw him sitting on the veranda.

"The boy looks fucked up," she snickered. "I think it's time you called."

✦

"Hey."

"K-Karma?"

"Yep."

Tony's hand was shaking. He pressed the phone tightly against his ear. "Karma Jackson?"

"Yes, Tony, it's me," Mildred said in a bored tone.

Tony's mouth went dry. For the past three days he'd kept expecting to open the paper and see the caption: "Unidentified Woman's Body Washes Ashore."

He hadn't slept for more than three or four hours, and every time he did feel an urge to eat he always ended up puking it right back up.

"I-I don't understand . . . Where are you?"

Mildred sighed. "I know. I should have called you sooner. I'm sorry, but I did want to tell you that I had a wonderful time."

Tony looked at the phone. The bitch must be crazy, he thought.

Truly puzzled, Tony repeated himself. "I don't understand."

"What?" Mildred said innocently. "I said I had a wonderful time."

Was he dreaming? Was she just going to ignore the fact that she'd left him there on the beach, naked?

"I woke up and you weren't there."

"Where?"

Yeah, she *was* crazy!

Tony tried to keep his tone calm, but it was a struggle. "On the beach. I woke up naked on the beach, and you weren't there. I thought you'd drowned!"

Mildred was quiet for a moment.

"You woke up on the beach? That's funny. I left you at the house and took a taxi back to my hotel."

Tony gave his head a violent shake. "What? What are you talking about?"

Mildred started to repeat herself: "I left you—"

"I heard what you said, I just don't know why you're saying it!"

"I'm saying it because it's true." Mildred's voice remained low, even. "We made love on the beach and it was beautiful, and then we walked down to your house. You tried to get me to stay, but I wouldn't, and so I tucked you into bed and called the cab—"

"Then where are my clothes!"

"I don't like to be yelled at, Tony. Please don't do that."

Tony grumbled, "Sorry."

"I put them in the washing machine. They were full of sand."

"You put them in the washing machine, huh?" Tony said as he marched back to the laundry room and flipped the lid of the machine up.

"Hello?" Mildred called. "Do you see them there?"

"Y-yeah."

Tony couldn't believe his eyes, so he reached in and pulled out first his boxers, then the pants, followed by the shirt.

"I put your wallet in the nightstand drawer, along with your watch and your keys."

He'd never in life been so fucked up that he couldn't remember anything he'd done the previous night.

But that still didn't explain why he woke up naked on the beach.

"But I don't understand," he said as he moved to the bedroom and opened the nightstand drawer. "How did I end up back on the beach?"

Mildred took a long moment before she replied. "Well, I've read that sometimes a heavy conscience can cause some people to sleepwalk."

CHAPTER

Fifty-seven

The next time they met, Tony pressed Mildred to tell him where it was she was staying. By then of course she and Chevy had decided that it would be better if Mildred moved into Chevy's bungalow, which sat down the road from the property grounds.

The kitchen was so small, one could barely turn around in it, but that didn't stop Mildred from preparing a lavish meal for Tony. Before either of them knew it, another two weeks had passed and Tony and Mildred were spending most of their free time together.

The murderous thoughts Mildred was having about Tony had begun to melt away and were replaced by fantasies of her living the rest of her life in Barbados as Karma Jackson . . . and maybe Karma Jackson-Landry.

She'd begun to make excuses as to why he'd done her the way he did. It was my fault, she told herself. I was fat, ugly, and desperate. She even fooled herself into believing that had she been in Tony's position, she would have done the same thing.

It wasn't until Chevy approached her about the Web sites Mildred had visited on her laptop that she was able to put things back into perspective.

"Hey," Chevy said as she stood outside Mildred's bedroom door.

"Hey," Mildred called back. She was checking her makeup in the small oval mirror that hung on the wall above the dresser.

"Going out with Tony again?"

"Yep."

"Uh-huh," Chevy said as she walked in and sat down on the edge of the bed. "You two are certainly spending a lot of time together."

"Yeah, I guess."

Chevy crossed her legs. "But you're still intending on breaking his heart, right?"

Mildred was gliding lipstick over her lips. She raised her eyes and caught a glimpse of the cynical expression on Chevy's face.

Her response was casual. "Of course."

"Really?"

Mildred turned around to face her. Placing one hand on her hip, she said, "What, you don't believe me?"

How could Chevy believe her when she didn't even believe herself?

"Well, I'm a little confused," Chevy started, looking thoughtfully down at her hands. "It seems as though you've been visiting a lot of Web sites that provide information for people who want to legally change their name."

"So, what's wrong with that?" Mildred said in a huff as she walked across the room and snatched her shawl from the corner chair. "I've changed my look—why not my name?"

Chevy continued to inspect her hands. "There's nothing at all wrong with that, but I also see that you've earmarked a site that gives information about just how long someone needs to be on the island before she can be legally wed here."

Mildred wrapped the shawl around her shoulders and then exploded in anger.

"That's my personal business!"

"Not if you pursue it on *my* computer, it's not."

"Why are you spying on me?"

"Why are you fooling yourself into believing that this man can love anyone besides himself?"

"He's changed."

"No, he hasn't."

"You don't know. He's not like that person he was back in New York. You're not with us—you don't know the things he says, and you don't see how he looks at me!"

Chevy sighed. Women can be so foolish, she thought as she slowly turned around and looked at Mildred, who was shaking all over with frustration.

"Don't you see, Mildred? He's telling you the same

thing he told you in New York, except now he's telling it to Karma Jackson."

Mildred was defiant. "Karma Jackson is not Mildred Johnson!"

Chevy rose from the bed, walked over to Mildred, and took her hand in hers. "Come here," she said as she led her back to the mirror.

Together they stood staring at their reflections. "You may not look in that mirror and see Mildred Johnson, but she's still there," Chevy said as she placed her hand on Mildred's chest and tapped her finger against her skin, "in there."

Mildred closed her eyes and tried to fight back the tears she knew would tell Chevy that she was right.

"So I think you have a few choices here: One, fess up and tell him who you really are. Two, pack your things, go home, and get on with your life. Or three, finish what you started out to do. But you have to make a decision, because fooling Tony is one thing, and after it's all said and done, he'll recover. But fooling yourself will leave you scarred for life."

CHAPTER

Fifty-eight

Mildred took Chevy's words to heart but told her that she had to think about things and that she would come to a decision over the next couple of days.

Now she and Tony watched as the concrete spilled out of the large rotating end of the truck. The day had finally arrived. The foundation of the house was being poured.

"Shit," Tony mumbled under his breath.

"What?" Mildred turned to him and asked.

Tony shook his head in amazement and he gave her hand a tender squeeze. "I can't believe it's finally happening," he said, his voice choked with emotion.

"Well, baby," she purred, turning to him and resting her cheek on his shoulder, "you've worked hard for it."

✦

Back at Tony's rental house, they lounged on the veranda, sipping champagne. They'd already consumed one bottle and now they were on their second and Tony was giddy with drunken happiness.

"You know, Karma," he started, leaning over and reaching for the bottle of bubbly, "I can't remember ever being so happy. So satisfied."

Mildred was wearing a cream and brown miniskirt, and Tony's eyes were temporarily lost in the curve of her thigh before he continued. "I never knew that I could feel this way about any place or . . . any person."

His eyes found hers and his gaze was penetrating.

"I don't know if it's this place or you or the combination of the two. I just know that I am so fucking happy and I don't want to be without this feeling . . . ever."

He was up on his feet, his hand stretched out to her.

"Take my hand, Karma."

Mildred slowly placed her hand in his. He gently pulled her up and to him. His hands were warm on her bare back.

"I love you, Karma."

Mildred closed her eyes. He had said it.

Tony had finally said it, and its legitimacy was evident in his tone and in his touch. Now that she had a comparison, she knew for sure that the first time had been a complete and utter lie.

"Did you hear me, Karma?" he asked as he pulled her closer to him. "I love you and I want us to be together forever."

Mildred pulled slightly away from him. His eyes were full of sincerity. And it was real this time, not the bootleg version.

Chevy was right. She had to make a decision.

"I love you too, Tony."

CHAPTER

Fifty-nine

You're a sick puppy, Chevy."

"No, I just know what the hell I'm doing."

Mildred stared at the wand.

"Where in the world did you get this?"

Chevy sighed. Mildred always asked too many questions.

"I have my sources."

"Eeewwww," Mildred cried, and shrank away as Chevy pushed the wand at her. "Someone has pissed on that! I don't want to touch it."

Chevy glared at her. "She didn't pee on the handle, stupid. Now take it!"

Mildred hesitated for a second more and then slowly

raised her hand and took the handle of the wand between her thumb and index finger.

"Don't drop it," Chevy warned. "Now, you know what to do?"

Mildred, still eyeing the wand with disgust, nodded.

"And you better make it believable!"

Mildred started toward the bathroom. How could she not make it believable? Who would guess that she'd gotten a hold of a used pregnancy test as a prop for her diabolical plan? Shit, she didn't even believe it.

Chevy looked at her watch. "Okay, I gotta go," she announced, walking toward the door. "Call me later, if you can."

Mildred laid the washcloth down on the sink edge and then rested the wand on the washcloth, before washing her hands three times in scalding water.

Moving back into the kitchen, she looked up at the clock. It was almost six. Tony would arrive in the next half hour or so. She didn't have much time to get a lie together.

But then, why worry? She had become a champion liar. Mildred supposed living a double life would do that to some people, but now she worried that she might even be pathological.

◆

"You ready?" asked Tony, rolling down the car window. Mildred had been waiting in the doorway for him.

"Well, yes and no." Mildred's face was laced with mischief.

"What's going on?"

"Nothing, really—I just need you to come inside for a second."

Tony's face went gray. "Is *she* in there?"

He didn't much like Chevy.

Mildred shook her head no.

Tony hesitated for a moment and then climbed out of the car. "Okay, but just for a minute."

Taking him by the hand, Mildred led him over to the couch and sat down beside him. She playfully knocked his thigh with her own.

"What's going on?"

"You love me?" Mildred asked.

Tony laughed, falling back into the cushions of the couch. "What, the forty times a day I tell you ain't enough?"

"Do you love me?"

"Okay, I love you for the forty-first time today!" Tony joyfully bellowed.

"Good," Mildred said, and then exhaled before folding her hands in her lap. Her expression went serious and Tony became concerned.

"What is it, baby—what do you need to tell me?"

"I-I think it's better if I showed you," Mildred said as she reached for the washcloth that sat on the sofa table. Slowly she unfolded the material.

Tony looked down at the long white piece of plastic. It took a minute for him to realize exactly what it was and then another minute to comprehend what the tiny green plus sign meant.

"Pregnant? You're pregnant?" he said unbelievingly.

Mildred nodded. "Are you happy?"

"But how . . . When . . . ? We're always safe. We use condoms."

Mildred rested her head on his shoulder. "That first night, on the beach, remember?"

It slowly came back to him.

"Oh, yeah. Wow."

"You didn't answer me, Tony."

"W-what?"

"Are you happy?"

He figured that if he wasn't in a state of shock he would be able to feel the happiness. He loved this woman, so that happiness had to be there, somewhere beneath the astonishment.

"Yes, yes, of course I am."

✦

They were both quiet as Tony guided the car around a shadowy curve. Lost in his thoughts, he tossed around his options and found that he had only one.

It was time to fess up to things. He was going to be a father.

A father? It sounded so strange to him.

He was going to have to be responsible for someone other than himself, and to tell the truth, that scared the shit out of him.

But what was done was done. He loved Karma—loved her laugh, her smile, her spirit, and the mystery that swirled all around her.

They were both on the same path, running from a former life. Tony supposed that made them a perfect match.

And it was true what she said about his conscience. It was heavy, and he didn't want to go into his new role with all of that heaviness—he would tell her about what he did back in New York and trust that if she loved him enough to carry his child, she loved him enough to carry his secret too.

CHAPTER

Sixty

Three days after Mildred announced her mock pregnancy to Tony, Chevy watched from the corner of the bedroom as Mildred packed her suitcase.

Chevy didn't know if this was the best thing for Mildred to do.

Moving in with the enemy?

Fucking him was one thing, deceiving him was another, but cohabitating could introduce a whole set of problems that neither one of them had factored in to the plan.

"I don't know, Mildred. I just think it might be a mistake."

Mildred flung outfit after outfit into the open suitcase.

"Oh, it's the right time, all right," she huffed as she

snatched open a dresser drawer and began tossing in her underwear.

Chevy cocked her head to one side. "Why are you so wound up then?"

Mildred shook her head in frustration. "You—you didn't hear what he said about Mildred—I mean, me."

Chevy's back straightened. "What did he say?"

Mildred stopped, her chest heaving. "He was so smug, so fucking smug about the entire thing—" Mildred stopped, wiped a tear from her cheek. "He was like, I did this thing in New York, something that I'm not proud of, but what's done is done and maybe it was destiny, because I met you and . . ."

Mildred paused again. Chevy could tell from the expression on her face that Mildred was replaying the entire scene in her head.

"I just can't believe it," she muttered.

"Believe what? What did he say?"

Mildred took a deep breath. "Well, he didn't seem to want to tell me the whole sordid story, but I pushed and he finally did." She took another deep breath. "He said that he'd used this woman to get ahead financially. I asked what the woman's name was and he said Mildred. I asked what did she look like, and he said she looked like a pig on steroids and every time he looked at her he felt sick to his stomach!"

Chevy's eyes popped.

"I told him that real beauty lies on the inside, and Tony said he wasn't interested in what was on the inside of Mildred Johnson."

Chevy stayed quiet.

"I said, 'Didn't you even care for her a tiny, itty-bitty bit?' and he said, 'Not one ounce'! And," Mildred barked, pointing her index finger up in the air, "he lied. He said that this whole thing happened years ago."

Chevy raised her eyebrows, "Really?"

"Yep. Years ago when he was still shallow and immature. And how he would never do anything like that now. Liar!"

Chevy smiled. "You see? A leopard doesn't change his stripes."

"Spots."

"What?"

"A leopard has spots, not stripes."

"Whatever," Chevy said, waving her hand. "A dog is still a dog."

CHAPTER

Sixty-one

He'd grabbed her as soon as she stepped into the house, then pressed her up against the wall and covered her face in kisses.

"Tony, wait." She laughed breathlessly as he dragged her to the bedroom.

"I've got to have you," he said as he began stripping her clothes from her body. "I've been thinking about you all day long." He used his teeth to pull her thong off.

Mildred giggled. She loved being ravished.

When he was naked he dove on top of her, taking her breasts into his mouth and sucking her nipples hungrily. Mildred reached down and took hold of his penis, expertly gliding her hand up and down the shaft until Tony thought he would burst.

"Put it in, baby, please," he begged.

Mildred eased him inside of her. She was sopping wet and Tony shivered with pleasure.

"Damn, baby . . . oh, baby . . ." Tony moaned into her ear as he pushed himself deeper inside her. "I love you, I love you," he mumbled into her neck.

Mildred had been working the hell out of those Kegel balls Chevy had given her, and it was paying off nicely.

She constricted her muscles.

"Aaah, stop it—you're going to make me come."

Tony pulled out a bit, raised himself up onto his arms, and gazed down at her. "I'm so glad you're here," he said before sinking into her again.

Mildred closed her eyes and began to grind her hips against him. She dug her finger into his waist, pulling him deeper.

They were both slick with perspiration by the time he started to approach his climax. He lunged into her with passionate fury. Sensing the approaching explosion, Mildred wrapped her legs around his back.

"I'm coming, baby, I'm coming," Tony screamed before his entire body exploded in convulsions.

Afterward, as they lay there basking in the afterglow of their lovemaking, Tony placed a gentle kiss on her cheek before climbing out of the bed and walking to the bathroom.

Mildred threw her arm over her forehead and gazed up at the whirling blades of the ceiling fan.

This would be so perfect, she thought to herself, if it wasn't so fucked up.

Tony reentered the room, his limp penis bouncing against his strong thigh. Coming to sit alongside her again, he took her hand in his, kissed her palm, her wrist, and then began to kiss the tips of her fingers.

Mildred watched him with quiet satisfaction. This is what real love looked like, felt like.

She closed her eyes as he gently sucked each of her fingers. She thoroughly enjoyed the eroticism of it.

As casually as he started, he stopped, and Mildred opened her eyes to see a sparkling diamond ring on her finger.

She was speechless.

"Karma, would you do me the honor of becoming my wife?" Tony's voice quaked. He moved from the bed and then got down onto his knees. Mildred raised herself up and into a sitting position as Tony gently rested his head on her stomach.

It should have been the sweetest moment in her life, but it was marred by the memory of his words: *She looked like a pig on steroids!*

Mildred's lips curled. "There's nothing in the world I would want more."

CHAPTER

Sixty-two

Tony opened the medicine cabinet and his eyes fell on his shaving cream, a box of Tylenol, and the bottle of prenatal pills. Closing the cabinet, he was met with his mirror image.

The mirror Tony grinned foolishly back at him.

"Baby?" Mildred called to him from the bedroom. "Do you need me to make you something before you go?"

They'd been living together for a month now and Mildred had gotten through her first menstrual cycle with tampons she kept hidden deep inside the box of laundry detergent. For the five days she bled, she claimed morning, afternoon, and evening sickness in order to keep him off her.

While Tony was out supervising the operation of his

Jet Skis, Mildred spent her time spending the money she had helped him steal. She was planning the most fabulous wedding the island had ever seen. They'd already booked the prestigious Sandy Lane Hotel, the same hotel where Tiger Woods had had his wedding.

Rock lobster, escargots, and caviar for the cocktail reception. A live band and horse-drawn carriage.

"A cup of tea?"

"Nah, I'm good," Tony called back as he reached in and started the shower.

She was already being the good wife. She waited on him hand and foot, laughed at all of his jokes, cooked fabulous meals for him, fucked him long and hard, and showered him with unconditional love.

Tony felt like he'd hit the jackpot.

And for the icing on the cake, the contractor had called just that morning to advise him that he and his team were ahead of schedule.

Could things get any better?

◆

Later that day, as Mildred and Chevy finished up their lunch, Chevy looked deep into her glass of iced tea as she pondered Mildred's next move. She didn't know if Tony trusted Mildred enough to go along with it.

Mildred had told Tony that she'd been in touch with her parents to tell them of her impending wedding and that even though she was estranged from them she was willing—for the sake of her new husband and unborn child—to try to work things out. During the conversation, her father had shared some confidential information with her, some information that would make them all rich. The investment was a mere $200,000, and the return would more than double within thirty days.

That last little tidbit had gotten Tony salivating.

"That's a lot of money to just hand over to someone you've never met before. Wouldn't he want to talk to your father first, to get the particulars?"

"Yeah, he did say he wanted to speak to him," Mildred said as her eyes roamed around the restaurant, as if seeking out someone right there who would carry out that part of the plan for her.

"Let me think about it and I'll call you later on tonight, okay?" Chevy announced as she stared off into the distance.

Mildred nodded.

CHAPTER

Sixty-three

Hello?"

"Noah?"

"Chevy?"

"Yep!"

"Well, Ms. Drama! How the hell are you?"

Noah's clipped Brooklyn-British accent echoed across the telephone line. The friendship between Chevy, Geneva, and Noah went back decades, back to a time when they all lived in an Upper West Side housing project. Now Noah lived in London with his partner, Zahn, and daughter, Destiny.

"If I complain, will you listen?" Chevy laughed into the phone.

"Probably not!" Noah exclaimed. "But I know you, Ms. Drama—it's not like you to make a long-distance call just to say hello. You're an e-mail type of girl, so let's cut through the bullshit and get down to the *real* shit, shall we?"

Chevy could hear Noah snapping his fingers in the background, and she imagined the snapping fingers were probably accompanied by a dramatic neck roll as well.

"Okay, Noah, you got me," Chevy allowed. "I need a favor."

"I ain't got no money—"

"I don't need any money, Noah. I need—"

"Good, because I got one child, not two, and—"

"Noah!"

"Look, Ms. Drama, don't be raising your voice at me—"

"Noah, please, will you let me speak? This is my dime, you know?"

Noah was silent for a minute.

"Well, go on, speak!"

"Okay . . ."

Chevy gave Noah the abridged version of what had happened, what was happening, and what they wanted to happen.

Noah laughed long and hard, and then he said, "I don't know, Miss Drama. That can't be good karma for me— excuse my pun." Noah giggled.

"Aw, c'mon, Noah," Chevy whined into the phone.

"Why should I?"

"Because we're friends."

"Yeah, you and I are friends. I don't know this Mildred chick from Adam!"

Chevy bit her lip. "But she's my friend, and Geneva's friend, which makes her your friend by association."

"That's all you could come up with?"

Chevy knew it was pitiful.

"Please," she said.

Noah released a heavy sigh.

"Will this be the last thing you ever ask me for?"

Chevy crossed her fingers. "Yes!"

Another sigh.

"Okay, then, give me the child's number. I'll call her tomorrow at this time."

"Thank you, Noah."

"Yeah, whatever. Now what is her pappy's name suppose to be again?"

CHAPTER

Sixty-four

Yes, sir." Tony grinned and nodded with the phone as he paced the living room.

Mildred sat on the edge of the couch, her legs folded beneath her as she chewed nervously on the cuticle of her thumb.

"Yes, Mr. Jackson, I understand that this is confidential information . . ."

Chevy's friend Noah had been on the phone with Tony for nearly an hour. Mildred had watched anxiously as Tony listened intently to what Noah was saying, and every now and again he'd rush to the table and jot down notes on the legal pad he'd placed there earlier.

Mildred thought that at any moment Noah would say something off-center, something that would trigger Tony's suspicion, and the jig would be up. But that never happened.

"Yes, sir. Thank you, sir. It was a pleasure speaking to you too, sir, and I look forward to meeting you as well."

Tony pressed End on the cordless phone before punching the air with his fist.

"Baby!" he cried ecstatically as he rushed toward Mildred and snatched her up, swinging her through the air. "We are going to be rich!"

He covered her face in kisses before setting her back down on the couch again. Looking down at his watch, he announced, "I gotta get down to the bank before it closes."

Mildred almost felt sorry for him as she watched him snatch up his car keys and rush out of the house.

"I love you, baby!" Tony shouted over his shoulder before jumping into the car and speeding off.

Mildred *almost* felt sorry for him, but then she heard his voice in her head saying: *She looked like a pig on steroids!*

And that small bit of pity vanished like a puff of smoke.

◆

Mildred was sitting outside on the veranda when she received the call from Chevy.

"Hello?"

"Well, it's done," Chevy advised in a conspiratorial tone.

Mildred said nothing.

"Noah called to say the money hit his account early this morning."

"Oh."

"He's going to issue you a cashier's check for the amount."

"How much was it again?"

"Two hundred thousand dollars."

Mildred shook her head in dismay. The money didn't mean anything to her. She'd trade it all in a minute for true love.

"You're rich, girl!" Chevy squealed.

"I guess." Mildred yawned.

CHAPTER

Sixty-five

Thirty days.

Thirty little days—that's all Tony would have to wait, and after those thirty days his two hundred Gs would multiply into half a million!

It was a sure thing, Karma's father, Mr. Jackson, had told him. The foreign currency market was usually a gamble, but this was a sure bet.

Tony didn't know anything about trading foreign currency, but he didn't need to. Karma's father was an expert, had made half of his fortune on the foreign currency market and had made the other half on the foreign currency *black* market!

Tony was on top of the world, and the pièce de résistance was just two days away. His wedding.

"It's almost one o'clock," Mildred called from the living room. "If we don't leave now, we're going to be late."

"Okay, babe," Tony called back to her as he quickly dabbed some cologne onto his neck.

They were going to pick up Errol and Tony's mother from the airport. Mildred had been sick to her stomach all day. She really hadn't wanted to involve anyone else in this mess, but what was she going to tell Tony, "Don't invite your mother and best friend"?

His sister wasn't going to be able to make it, and that was just fine with Mildred. One less person she had to look in the eye and lie to.

At the airport, Mildred sat on a bench, sipping a ginger beer, while Tony paced the tiled floor of the Arrivals section.

It was obvious that he was bursting with excitement, and when he finally spotted his mother and Errol coming through the door, he bolted toward them. For a minute, Mildred thought he was going to leap into Errol's arms, but at the last moment he stopped short and threw his arms around him in a manly embrace.

He gave his mother a stiff hug and an awkward peck on the cheek before pulling her straw bag from her hands and starting off toward Mildred.

Mildred stood, smoothed her light blue linen skirt, and fixed her face with a bright smile.

Tony was babbling a mile a minute as he pointed proudly at Mildred. Mrs. Landry's face broke out into an approving smile, while Errol's expression was a mixture of bewilderment and . . . recognition?

"Mom, Errol," Tony said, wrapping his arm around Mildred's shoulder, "this is Karma Jackson."

Mrs. Landry's smile broadened as she shoved Tony aside and threw her beefy arms around Karma and squeezed. "Oh, child, so nice to finally meet you," she said, and then stepped back. "What a beautiful woman you are." She was beaming.

"Thank you," Mildred said.

Errol stepped forward and presented his hand. "I concur," he said as he eyed Mildred closely, "but why do I have the feeling we've met before?"

Mildred dropped her eyes. "I-I don't know. I guess I just have one of those faces."

"Yeah, I felt that way too," Tony said as he started toward the parked car.

✦

They stopped in at the Blue Monkey to get a late lunch. Mildred had been quiet most of the trip from the airport. She and Tony's mother sat in the backseat, while Errol and Tony sat up front. Every now and again, Errol would turn around and gaze at her in a way that made Mildred uncomfortable. She was sure he knew and would blow the whistle on her at any second.

Now they sat across from one another, each of them devouring a Chicken Roti.

"So when is my grandbaby due?" Ethel Landry said as she gave Mildred's tummy an affectionate pat.

"Oh, not until February," Mildred lied.

"Do you want a boy or a girl?"

"Doesn't matter—just as long as I have a healthy baby," Mildred said, staring down at her plate.

"Well, if it's a boy, you'll have to name him Anthony Junior, of course!"

"Now, Mom, we'll name him whatever we decide to name him," Tony intervened as he reached across the table and took Mildred's hand in his.

Ethel smirked and called for another beer.

✦

"You're not staying here?" Mrs. Landry yawned on the living room couch after Mildred bent over and kissed her lightly on the cheek.

"No, I'm going to stay with my girlfriend until the wedding day."

"Oh, no—are we putting you out?"

"No, no, of course not." Mildred patted the woman's hand. "I'll see you on Saturday, okay?"

"Of course, dear."

Errol was seated at the dining room table, flipping through the *Nation* newspaper. He looked up as Mildred rushed past him. "Hey, don't I get a goodbye?" he asked in an amused tone.

Mildred stalled, then turned and smiled. "Of course. I'm sorry, just real tired," she said, and then bent down and kissed him lightly on the cheek. "See you Saturday."

"Yeah, Saturday," Errol said as he watched her walk out to the car. "Something's just not right," Errol mumbled to himself.

"What was that, Errol?" Mrs. Landry called from the couch.

"Nothing."

CHAPTER

Sixty-six

What's wrong with you?"

Mildred was sulking. Sitting in a chair in the corner of Chevy's room, she had her feet propped up on the edge of the windowsill, her arms folded across her breasts, and her lip stuck out like a five-year-old who had had her favorite toy taken away.

She'd gone over to the house that morning when she knew Errol, Tony, and his mother would be indulging themselves at the Sandy Lane Spa and gathered up the rest of her clothes. On the center of the bed she'd left a note, even though Chevy had advised against it.

"Snap out of it, girl," Chevy cried, clapping her hands loudly together. "This is the pièce de résistance. This is what we—I mean, you—have worked so hard to accomplish."

Mildred knew that was the truth, but it was still her wedding day, and she'd planned the perfect wedding! And maybe it wouldn't be affecting her so badly if the day hadn't turned out to be so beautiful. Not a cloud lingered in that pale blue sky.

"Don't you feel good?" Chevy screeched, throwing her hands in the air. "I know I feel great," she added before doing a little victory dance across the room.

Mildred didn't feel good at all; she felt like she'd been cheated out of two weddings in one year. That had to be some kind of record.

"Whoo-wee," Mildred cried unenthusiastically as she spun her index finger in the air.

Chevy shook her head. "C'mon, girl, let's get you to the airport."

✦

They weren't expecting many guests, just a few guys Tony had befriended and their significant others; Karma's parents, who were supposed to have flown in very late the night before; Tony's mother and Errol; and of course Chevy.

On the beach outside the Sandy Lane Hotel, twenty chairs laced in shimmering white toule awaited the thirty or so guests. A baby grand piano had been rolled out onto the beach, and Tony watched from the balcony of his hotel suite as the workers unfurled the lavender silk walkway.

"Are you nervous?" Errol asked, coming up beside him.

Tony shook his head. "I've never been more calm in my life," he said, his voice filled with amazement.

"Wow, man. I never thought I'd see the day when you'd settle down." Errol's voice was tinged with envy.

"Me neither, man, me neither," Tony said as he turned and walked back inside.

He reached for the telephone. He just wanted to hear her voice before they said "I do." He'd called three times and had only gotten voice mail at the hotel room as well as on her cell phone.

"Relax, man," Errol said as he handed him a glass of champagne. "She'll be there."

The sun was due to set at exactly 6:22 P.M., just as the preacher would instruct Tony to kiss his bride. It was 6:10 and Karma still had not made an appearance. Tony was beginning to feel sick to his stomach, but he smiled assuredly at his guests, who were fidgeting in their seats.

"She'll be here," Tony muttered nervously as he checked his watch again.

Errol had whispered in his ear that he would go and check to see if maybe she was sick or just had the last-minute jitters.

When Tony saw Errol returning—alone—he knew the unimaginable was happening.

Errol walked up to Tony, somber-faced, and turned

him away from the crowd. For a moment their eyes lit on the setting sun. It was a brilliant, fiery orange.

"Tony," Errol started, his voice choked with emotion, "she never checked in to the hotel."

CHAPTER

Sixty-seven

Errol clapped Tony on the back. "I'm sorry, man. Really, I am," he said as Tony shoved the key into the lock.

Tony was in a state of shock, but he could still feel the pain pulling at him. He was hurting like a son of a bitch; he'd never known heartbreak and knew for sure he'd never want to know it again. He'd held back the tears for most of the ride, but now he felt them coming on like a rainstorm.

"I just don't understand," his mother kept mumbling. "Why would she do something like this? She seemed like such a nice girl."

Tony left them in the living room and walked to the bedroom to peel himself out of his tuxedo. He would take a long hot shower, and while the water beat down on him, he'd cry his heart out.

What have I done to deserve this? he wondered as he unclasped his cuff links.

He sat down on the bed and dropped his head into his hands. He felt ill. He was sure that Karma was wherever his $200,000 had gone. And what of his unborn child? Was there really a baby? He didn't know anything anymore.

His stomach turned over and he rushed to the bathroom and puked into the toilet.

He was broke. Flat broke.

Returning to the bedroom, he noticed for the first time the envelope lying in the center of the bed.

Tony reached for it. His hands were shaking so badly, he could hardly get the envelope opened.

Dear Tony,

I have done to you the exact thing you did to me a year ago. I manipulated you in every way, shape, fashion, and form, used you for my own reward— revenge.

It's true what they say about karma—it's a bitch.

Mildred

Tony was confused as he stared down at the letter and the signature.

Mildred?

Had Mildred found him?

No, wait—she said she'd manipulated him.

Tony pressed his thumbs into his temples. He was losing his mind.

He tossed the envelope back down onto the bed and two passport-size photos tumbled out.

He recognized both women. One was Mildred Johnson and the other was the love of his life, Karma Jackson.

He still didn't understand.

Did they know each other? Had they conspired to rob him of his dignity and his money?

He held the pictures up close to his face and then something in him told him to flip the pictures over.

Scrawled behind the Mildred Johnson picture was: *Mildred Johnson—Before.*

Tony knew, before he even flipped the second picture over what was written there: *Mildred Johnson—After.*

He screamed then. Screamed and flew into a rage that didn't subside until every stick of furniture in the house was broken.

CHAPTER

Sixty-eight

Clutching a glass of champagne, Mildred stared out the tiny window of the first-class cabin.

She was finally headed home.

Sighing, she reached for the airplane telephone, swiped her credit card down its side, and dialed.

"Hello?"

"Geneva?"

"Mildred?"

"Yes, it's me."

"Are you okay?"

"I'm fine now."

"Where are you?"

"On my way home."

"Oh, good. That crazy-ass Chevy wasn't giving me

any information, and every time I dialed your number, you didn't pick up. I didn't know what in the world was going on—"

"I'll tell you all about it when I get home."

"Okay, then."

"Bye."

Mildred hung up and took a sip of her drink.

" 'Scuse me, miss?"

Mildred turned her head and came face-to-face with a gorgeous olive-skinned hunk of a man with the greenest eyes and the blackest hair she'd ever seen.

"Sorry to bother you, but I had to come over to tell you that you are stunning."

Mildred blushed.

"My name is Sergio Martinelli," he said, taking her hand and planting a kiss on it.

"Mil—I mean, Karma Jackson," Mildred replied.

"May I?" Sergio asked, indicating the empty seat beside her.

Mildred nodded.

"Do you live in New York?"

"Yes, I do. And you?"

"Me, I live in Italy," Sergio said, leaning in close. "The land of *amore*."

Mildred smiled and took a sip of her champagne.

"Are you married, Karma?"

"No, I'm not."

"Boyfriend?"

Mildred shook her head no.

Sergio clutched his chest. "God has finally smiled

down on Sergio Martinelli," he announced dramatically. "Would I be being too forward if I invited you to my home in Pisa?"

Mildred cocked her head to one side. What the hell did she have to lose? Mildred Johnson had lived her life. Now it was Karma Jackson's turn.

"No." Mildred grinned. "You wouldn't be forward at all."

GRATITUDE

Once again, thank you all for digging into your purses and wallets to support a sistah who's just trying to have her say!

I'm especially grateful to my editors, Phyllis Grann and Karen Marcus, publicist Tommy Semosh, as well as everybody at Random House who continues to support and promote the Geneva Holliday series.

Love and appreciation to my family, friends, and fans.

Hope to see you all here next year . . . I'll be easy to spot. Just look for the sistah with flaming red locks, round hips, full lips, holding that novel with the sexy cover.

Until then, remember . . . if you truly believe it in your heart, the universe will deliver.

Joy!

Geneva